ISOBELLE CARMODY

THE ICE MAZE

The Kingdom of the Lost

BOOK 3

PUFFIN BOOKS

Also by Isobelle Carmody

This book is for my dear friend Nan McNab,
warm and ever-welcoming wayside refuge
for this weary wanderer.

PUFFIN BOOKS

UK | USA | Canada | Ireland | Australia
India | New Zealand | South Africa | China

Penguin Books is part of the Penguin Random House group of companies
whose addresses can be found at global.penguinrandomhouse.com.

Penguin
Random House
Australia

First published by Penguin Random House Australia Pty Ltd, 2017.
This paperback edition published by Penguin Random House Australia Pty Ltd, 2020.

Design by Marina Messiha © Penguin Random House Australia Pty Ltd
Illustrations by Isobelle Carmody
Printed and bound in Australia by Griffin Press,
an accredited ISO AS/NZS 14001 Environmental Management Systems printer.

National Library of Australia Cataloguing-in-Publication data:

ISBN 978 0 143 78748 8 (paperback)

A catalogue record for this
book is available from the
NATIONAL
LIBRARY
OF AUSTRALIA
National Library of Australia

penguin.com.au

one

THE
FLYWAY

1

Redwing floated like an ember against the pale grey sky, the great scarlet and black sweep of her wings so beautiful that it seemed to Bily that a hand reached into his chest and squeezed his heart. Yet he wished she had not taken flight. It was a reminder that, all too soon, she would leave them, winging her way West through the high mountain passage the diggers called the flyway.

Without wings, he, Zluty, the injured Monster and the little diggers accompanying them had no choice but to continue along the feet of the great jagged line of mountains until they reached the end. Only then could they too turn West.

Seeing Zluty striding along with Flugal, bending his head to listen to the he digger, Bily thought about when they first met the diggers. Zluty had been unable to quieten his mind enough to hear the meaning of their words, let alone to understand and use the gestures that were part of their language. Now they were so accustomed to using digger words and gestures that they often spoke to one another that way.

Bily admired Zluty's yellow fur, that shone so boldly bright and warm in a world turned chill and colourless.

It was strange that the desert they had crossed to reach the mountains had been white, yet the dazzling sunlight and blue sky had contrived to turn shadows pooled in the lee of the dunes, deepest indigo and blue and violet, and at sunset, the white dune tips blushed pink and red and gold. Even the moon-shadows had been shifty greens and blues.

But the stone-studded black plain that stretched along the mountain range seemed to swallow the light rather than reflect it, and the sky was always cast over with a milky veil that never let them get a glimpse of the blue beyond. At night it hid the moon and stars, so that they had been unable to travel except in daylight. This slowed them badly, because the days had grown shorter since they'd left the digger settlement.

On the plain where they had lived in their cottage, the days got shorter in Winter, too, but the sky had been blue and the sun shone down, even if it lacked warmth. Here, at the foot of the mountains, day was no more than the time it took the veiled sun to rise a little way above the horizon, move in a short flat arc from East to West, and sink from sight again. Semmel said the days would go on getting shorter until there was no day at all. Only night.

'The Longful Night,' she said, adding in gesture that the dark was needful because from it would be born *the world's dream*.

Bily had no idea what *the world's dream* was. He and Zluty called the smaller blue moon that appeared and trailed after the moon for part of the year, the Moon's Dream, so perhaps the diggers meant the first rising of the Moon's Dream after the Winter.

Bily had dreamed of the Moon's Dream the night before, but the small moon had been grey. He had been dreaming strange, colourless dreams ever since leaving the digger settlement to travel North. Sometimes he heard the voice of the egg that had spoken inside his head when he and Zluty had first hatched. He could never remember what it had said when he woke, but the colourless dreams unsettled him. He did not like the idea that he might have to endure more of them. Yet what choice did he have? They must go North in order to get around the mountains, and maybe his dreams would be like that until they turned West.

He would not have minded if he had not been so hungry for colour. The world was all black and white and grey now, save for the brightness of Zluty's yellow fur, the flash of Redwing's scarlet feathers, the crimson canopy of the wagon, when it was not covered in cold fluffs or sodden to darkness. He missed the multitude of colours in his garden, the many hues of feather of the birds that had visited the cottage. Sometimes he opened his feather collection just to remember how many colours there were in the world.

It was a pity his fur and the digger pelts were the same colourless hues as the land and sky. Even the Monster, whose pelt was a lovely deep purple-brown at the paw and tail and ear tips, the rest of it a warm creamy colour, had been turned to shades of grey by the thin, cold light.

Bily looked down at his fur and thought the light made it look grubby, too. Then he frowned.

'What is it, *Bee-lee*?' Semmel asked, making the little twitching gesture towards him with her paw that meant *'you who are not part of the Makers plan'*.

'It is my fur,' Bily told her. 'I think it is getting thicker.'

The digger nodded calmly. 'That is happening when fur is getting too much coldness,' she said.

Bily studied Zluty, whose fur was shorter and coarser than his own, and was sure *it* had got thicker, too. He wondered if their fur would go on thickening the whole time they travelled into the frozen North. If so, he would end up being a giant fluff ball! The thought would have made him laugh, except it was very odd to think of his pelt growing all by itself without him having anything to say about it, just as if it had a mind of its own.

He glanced backwards, wondering what would have happened if they had followed the mountains in the other direction, towards the hot South. Would his fur have decided there was no need for itself at all, and fallen out? How very strange he and Zluty would look all bare and pink. Though Flugal had said their fur would singe if they went anywhere near the burning lakes in the South. Even the steaming smoke that came from them was poisonous to breathe.

Bily's gaze shifted to the mountains. Sometimes they seemed to him a great forbidding wall that the land had thrown up to bar their way. They could have gone over the mountains using the Monk's

lifting device, but they would have had to go at once and very quickly, for ice blizzards plagued the mountains in Winter, the soft cold fluffs turning into hard, sharp little fragments of ice that flew in the wind like knives. No living creature could be outside and survive a bad ice blizzard.

The main reason they had not crossed the mountains was that they would have had to leave their wagon behind, for beyond the Monk stronghold of Stonehouse was terrain where it could not be wheeled or dragged. And leaving the wagon would have meant leaving the Monster behind.

Bily had desperately wanted Redwing to go the

long way around with them so they could all stay together, but the diggers warned she would not survive the frozen Northland ahead. He comforted himself that as soon as they got around the end of the mountains, they would be able to travel back along the other side until they reached the place where the Western river flowed out, then follow it to the Vale of Bellflowers, where they would make a new home.

The thought of a new cottage made Bily happy, but he wondered if Redwing would be waiting in the Vale of Bellflowers when they got there, or if the call to fly West would take her ever farther away. He could not bear to think that he might never see her again. If only the pass through the mountains had not been blocked, they would be there already. But then Bily would not have met the terrible and sorrowful Cloud Monster, and he and Zluty would never have come to know Flugal and his clever digger clan; nor would they have learned about the Monks and their masters – the mysterious, malevolent Makers who dwelt on the other side of the sky crack.

Bily looked up again. Redwing had flown out of sight, but he was not looking for her now. He was thinking about the sky crack. When the diggers had first mentioned it, he had thought they meant a crevice atop the mountains, close to the sky. It was only later that he understood they had meant there was a crack *in* the sky. He did not like to think of the sky being cracked, let alone talk of it, but Zluty was so very curious about it that, when he was not offering Bily his theories about how it had come to be cracked in the first place, he was constantly questioning the diggers about it.

Zluty had also tried questioning the Monster about the sky crack, for its ancestors had also been sent through it, but the Monster had only woken twice since they left the digger encampment and both times its mind had been clouded with confusion. Of course, even when its mind was clear, it seldom answered questions.

Zluty's most recent theory was that the crack had occurred during whatever great upheaval had caused the land to lurch into mountains and the plain to crack into fissures and crevices. Bily could imagine the mountains heaving up so violently that one of them bumped into the sky, cracking it.

He noticed thick, dark grey clouds beginning to spill over the jagged mountain peaks and roll down towards them. The colour meant that soon cold fluffs would begin to fall again. They had been falling on and off ever since they had left the digger settlement, but although they sometimes covered the ground, turning it white for a time, the cold fluffs quickly melted, leaving puddles and only a few deeper patches of white that stayed. The diggers called the fluffs *coldwhites* but the Monks had called them by a Maker word: *snow*.

Bily liked to think of the Makers even less than he liked to think of the sky crack, for it was they who had sent the terrible stone storm machine that had destroyed their cottage. It was supposed to destroy everything because the Makers wanted nothing that was not of their own making when they came through the sky crack. If the diggers had not rebelled against their masters and damaged the machine, they would have got their wish. Neither the Monster nor the diggers had been able to say what a Maker looked like, save that they were too big to fit through the sky crack without it being made bigger. That was why they sent all the metal machines and devices and diggers and Monks and Monster's people through – for some reason the sky crack could not be made bigger from *their* side.

When Bily had nightmares about the Makers tearing open the sky, they always looked like the dreadful *slish* that had pursued Zluty in the crevice in the white desert when he had gone looking for water. He looked at the wagon for comfort. It was the closest thing they had to a home now, though it had begun as a humble means of hauling supplies back to the cottage. Zluty had made it out of a piece of the big silvery grey metal egg from which they had hatched. He had strengthened it to carry the injured Monster and their supplies when they set off in search of a new home after the stone storm crushed the cottage and poisoned their well – the same stone storm that had driven the Monster into the blackclaw nest and caused the rockfall that blocked the mountain pass.

'Everything is linked to everything else,' Bily murmured, and had the queer feeling he had heard the words somewhere before, perhaps in one of his dreams.

He went back to admiring the wagon, which had got very splendid because of changes wrought by the diggers. Not only had they enlarged it by building a rim, they had created clever shelves and storage niches. They had even cut a door into the

side, which they had decorated with tiny coloured tiles, and replaced the simple wooden frame with a light, strong metal frame. The new woven canopy had sections that could be rolled tightly and tied up or drop down either side, turning the wagon into a small cloth hut on wheels. Parts of the frame could fold out so that the cloth curtains could also be spread over them, offering shelter alongside the wagon. Bily and Zluty and the diggers laid their mattresses under the side canopies when they slept, so as not to wake covered in cold fluffs.

In addition to the things the diggers had done to the wagon, they had also bestowed on the travellers food for their journey and many other useful gifts, including a large and mysterious device lashed to the side of the wagon, consisting of metal poles, flat planks and a complex web of thongs and cloth. The diggers had steadfastly refused to explain what it was, save to say that they would need it in the North.

Bily was not sure how the diggers could know what would be needed in the North, since no living digger had travelled further than the flyway. Some of the first rebel diggers that destroyed the stone storm machine had fled North and had stayed there for some time before returning to build the current settlement. Strangely, these travellers had almost no memory of what had happened in the North, but they had brought back scent memories that yielded some information. To unlock the rest, the scent memories had to be carried North again.

When he spoke of it to Zluty, his brother said sturdily that they only had to get to the end of the line of mountains and how difficult could that be anyway?

But the scent memory picture he had seen in Semmel's mind showed that the mountain range did not end neatly. It curved East in a low arc of broken white-capped hills and mist-wreathed ice mounds that stretched out into a vast expanse of water. They would have to get beyond the broken arc before they could go West, and he had the feeling they would need the guidance of the memory scents.

'Do not be fearful,' the she digger had soothed, no doubt smelling Bily's anxiety. 'As we go Northly, the memory scents will be giving up more and more of their secretiveness.'

Suddenly, the wagon jerked to a halt. Bily trotted round the front after Zluty, only to see both front wheels were sunk in a furrow full of water. There was a little flurry of consternation from the diggers who had been pulling the towropes as they all came to look.

2

Zluty knelt and felt around in the water, trying to ignore the horrible wetness seeping through his fur. He had feared one of the wheels had got trapped in a fissure, but he could not feel a crack. Indeed, the ground had got a good deal smoother now that they were moving North, which was why he had not been paying proper attention.

'What is it?' Bily asked worriedly. 'Is a wheel broken?'

Zluty sat back on his heels and looked up into his brother's anxious face, marvelling how fluffy he had got in the misty air. 'There is a layer of ice under the melted water and the wheels can't get a grip when they turn. We need to lay down some stones.'

At Flugal's command, the diggers hastened away to search for small stones. Zluty got to his feet.

'You are all wet,' Bily said anxiously.

'Only my legs and arms,' Zluty replied, marvelling that Bily was fretting about him getting a bit wet when he had once dived his whole self under water. Bily would not agree that he had been brave, of course. He saw only that he had been very frightened but that what he had done had been needful.

Yet surely being brave *was* doing what was needful even though you were frightened?

The diggers returned with many small rocks, but none small enough, so they got out their little hammers and a flat, round metal plate and began to pound the small stones into smaller ones.

'Shall I make something hot for us to drink while we wait?' Bily asked. 'Then you could use the rest of the water to wash the mud off.'

Zluty hesitated. He knew it comforted his brother to prepare food but he did not want to stop so soon after they started. 'I'll brush the mud out later when it is dry,' he said. 'Flugal says that if we don't hurry, we will not reach the flyway by dusk tomorrow, and Redwing would have to go through it in the dark.'

'She could wait until morning,' Bily said eagerly.

'She would have to wait the whole night and another day, for Flugal says dusk is the proper time to go through. That is when the light shines through the flyway from the West and the wind blows from the East.' He hesitated, then added, 'And you know, she might not be able to wait.'

Bily's face fell.

'She can't help going,' Zluty said gently, patting his brother's shoulder.

'I know.' Bily wrung his hands. 'It's only . . . I don't know why she must go now. She never wanted to go with the other birds who always flew West from the cottage when Winter came, but now she wants so badly to go. Yet she does not know what calls her.'

Zluty did not know what to say. It was true that Redwing had never flown far from the cottage when they had lived on the plain. Her longing to fly West had begun only after they left the ruined cottage, and it had got stronger every day they travelled. Now it was so powerful that it filled her mind, and when Zluty tried to talk to her, it beat against his mind, too, filling him with a strange urgent impatience.

When the diggers had created enough grit stone, Zluty laid it in front of the wheels. Zluty did not admit he was worried that even with all of them

helping they might not be able to get the wagon out of the furrow without first getting the Monster out. Aside from causing it discomfort, that would delay them, and Redwing's flight was not the only reason Zluty was concerned about getting on as fast as they could.

Flugal had warned him that the memory scents told that in Winter in the North, deadly ice blizzards came down from the mountains. They must get around the end of the range before the ice blizzard season began, or they would have to find shelter and wait until Winter ended before they could go on.

Zluty had no idea where they would find shelter in the frozen North. And even if the memory scents did lead them to a cave where they could take refuge, they would soon run out of fuel to burn and food to eat. He scowled and pushed away the thought of being trapped in a cave and hungry, reminding himself that the diggers who rebelled against the Makers had fled North and survived. Even if the memory scents of those early diggers failed them, Zluty *would* find food and something to burn, just as he had always done.

He would not tell Bily about the ice blizzards.

His soft-hearted brother was upset enough about being parted from Redwing. There was no need for him to be burdened by knowledge of a danger they might never encounter.

Once Zluty had pushed the stone grit under and about the submerged wheels, he and Bily put their shoulders to the wagon and shoved, while the diggers pulled on the towropes.

It did not budge.

'Again!' Zluty shouted, and this time when he shoved, the wagon lurched forward slightly. Zluty cried out urgently to the diggers to keep pulling, as he and Bily heaved again. The wagon moved forward and bumped up, and just like that the front wheels were free of the sodden furrow. When they

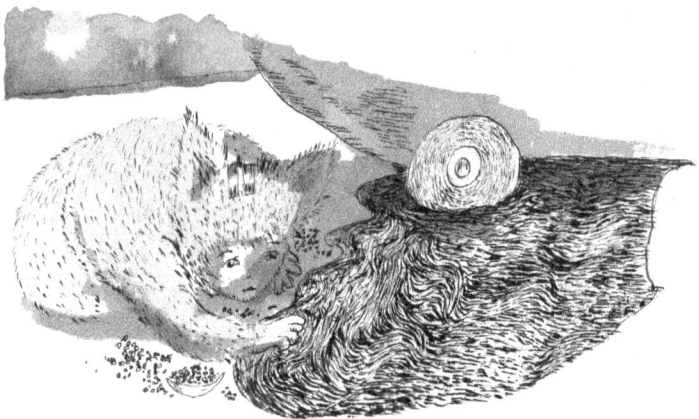

had pushed the back wheels through it and out, some of the diggers gave a ragged little *Ra!*

But Flugal shook his head when they were walking beside the wagon again. 'It is a bad sign,' he said gloomily.

'*What* is?' Zluty asked him.

'Freezingness at the bottom of the puddle,' the he digger answered. 'The memory scents tell that it signals the coming of a badful Winter.'

Very coldful will be the long night of Winter, he added in gestures.

Zluty wondered if the digger meant that ice blizzards only came in the night. He was still not as good as Bily at reading the gestures that were part of the diggers' language, and sometimes he got very muddled about what was being said.

'Why did the rebel diggers go North after they destroyed the stone storm machine, if it was so difficult and dangerous there?' he asked.

'Only some went,' Flugal said. 'We do not have the knowing of why, but Monks hating cold and Wintertime dark – they staying inside Stonehouse all the dark nights. They never going North.'

'Why didn't the diggers who came back lead everyone else North, then?' Zluty asked.

'Not having that knowing,' Flugal said again. 'Maybe knowing will come from memory scents when we are further Northly. Leader of diggers is wanting that knowing. Semmel will gathering them to take back.'

'So you are not just coming with us to free the Cloud Monster?' Zluty asked, not sure how he felt that the digger leader had not mentioned this other secret task, though the Cloud Monster *had* saved his life.

'Freeing of Cloud Monster is debt of honour,' Flugal said gravely. 'But gathering of knowing is also important.'

Bily climbed up onto the back of the wagon to check on the Monster. He was relieved to see it was still sound asleep despite the bumping and shouting. It needed sleep, because even though the blackclaw bite that had so nearly killed it was healing – thanks to a special mixture that had been brewed up by the potion-maker in the digger camp – the Monster was far from well. Aside from being terribly weakened by being poisoned, there was something wrong with the Makers metal inside it.

At first the diggers had thought it must be damaged, but after examining the Monster, the digger potion-maker said its metal was ailing because it had got too far from the Makers machines in the Velvet City. The potion-maker had given the Monster a potion to soothe its metal, but warned that it would not be properly healed until it returned to the Velvet City. After drinking the draught, the Monster had fallen asleep and had not been properly awake and alert since.

This was a good thing, because it had clearly been a shock to the Monster to learn it was bound to the Makers machines. It had told Bily and Zluty proudly that its people served the Makers of their own free will, and were beloved of them, but now it knew that to be a lie. It was bound to the Makers machines just as the diggers were, the binding shaped to prevent it straying too far and too long from the Velvet City.

Bily wondered if any other Listeners knew the truth. He thought it unlikely, since the Monster said its people seldom left the City.

What would they do when they discovered their health depended on them staying close to the Velvet City and the Makers machines? Surely they would mind very much, as the Monster did. Unless they did not believe the Monster.

It never had given them a proper reason for leaving the city, save to say that it had not wanted something it was to be given. But it had not really run away. The Monster had said it had gone to the white desert to think, and had been overtaken by the stone storm, the *arosh*. That had driven it down from the mountains and across the white desert to the plain where he and Zluty lived, where it had been bitten by the blackclaw. Yet it seemed to Bily the Monster had never shown any great desire to return to the Velvet City, though that might have been because it had thought it would die.

Gazing into its enormous sleeping face, Bily suddenly found himself wondering *how* the Monster and the diggers had got Makers metal inside them.

Of course the Makers had put it into the first diggers they sent through the sky crack, but now diggers mated and gave birth to digger younglings in their burrows and never saw a Maker. It must be that a bit of Makers metal passed like a seed from the she digger to her younglings when they were inside her. And that tiny bit of Makers metal did nothing – unless the Monks caught a digger and

took them to the Makers machines in Stonehouse.

As for the Monks, Bily supposed they came in eggs like he and Bily had done, since he had seen no she Monks or younglings in Stonehouse. The metal in them must instantly bond to the Makers machine when they emerged from their eggs.

The Monster had said enough of the Listeners for Bily to know that its kind were born of one another like diggers, so perhaps they, too, passed on metal to their younglings which bonded to the Makers machine at their birth. But it must be such a light bond that they did not notice it unless they went too far from the Velvet City. He wondered at the purpose of such a bond, and could only suppose the Makers wanted the Listeners to concentrate on helping to widen the sky crack.

The diggers had told them that the Makers machines and devices were intended to widen the sky crack so the Makers could fit through, but they did not know how that widening was being done, save that it had something to do with the Makers machine in the Velvet City, and with the Monks in Stonehouse atop the mountains.

Bily did not care why the Makers wanted to come through the sky crack. He only hoped that they would never manage it.

The Monster opened its eyes and, caught in its fierce gaze, Bily was reminded of the first time he had seen those yellow, seed-shaped eyes glowing in the darkness of the cottage cellar. Then, he had been certain the Monster meant to eat him. Now, he was only relieved to see that its eyes were completely clear for the first time since they had left the diggers camp.

3

Bily reached out and stroked the Monster's silky pelt, a thing he would not once have dared do, wishing he might brush it.

'Your fur has got so thick,' he murmured.

The Monster lifted its head.

'Because of the cold.' It said the words inside his mind, dark and soft. 'It happens to the Listeners sent to carry message eggs to Stonehouse when they travel near to Winter. But the thickness falls out when they return because it is so hot in the Velvet City.'

'You ought to go back to sleep,' Bily said gently,

hoping he had not broken the soothing thrall of the potion. 'I'm sorry I woke you.'

The Monster's eyes went beyond him to the opening in the awning. 'We are travelling North,' it said, nostrils quivering.

It was not a question, but Bily nodded. 'It is the only way to get around the mountains.'

'North,' the Monster said again, as if tasting the word.

'Do you remember in the digger settlement, I said you need not return to the Velvet City?' Bily asked. The Monster's eyes turned back to him, and he added quickly, 'Of course you must go there to get your metal soothed, but I meant that you need not stay if you don't want. Once your metal is better, you can come with us to the Vale of Bellflowers. I can take care of you until you are strong again, then you can go where you like.'

'Can I?' the Monster asked coldly. 'It seems I have no choice, since I am bound to the Makers machine in the Velvet City.'

'But you *chose* to leave the Velvet City in the first place, so it mustn't be a very strong binding.'

'I did not choose to leave. I was driven away by the *arosh*,' the Monster said. 'I was afraid.'

'Maybe it was being afraid that let you choose,'
Bily said. 'After all, the diggers were bound to the
Makers until they got angry at the destruction of
Redwing's people. Maybe it was their anger that let
them break the machine and run away. Maybe if
you get angry you will be able to leave again.'

The Monster gave him a long look. 'Comings
and goings in the Velvet City are no simple matter,
Bily. There are rules about who can go where and
when. You and Zluty should leave the river before
it reaches the Velvet City, and circle around the
settlement before returning to the river to follow
it West.'

It laid its head down and closed its eyes.

Bily knew it was not sleeping, but he said nothing. He had no intention of letting the Monster go into the Velvet City on its own. Aside from all else, it might be too weak to walk that far. But there was a long journey ahead of them in which he would have time to think of an argument that would change its mind. Certainly Zluty would agree that they could not abandon it. The trouble was that his intrepid brother was likely to want to go into the Velvet City *with* the Monster.

Bily noticed a small web woven between two bits of the frame under the awning in a little protected corner, and he studied the intricate net with pleasure. Spiders were such wonderful weavers and he always felt a fellow feeling for them.

There was no sign of the spider, but a leaf caught at the warmest corner had been woven around and around with gossamer. Bily sent a whispered greeting with his mind into the curled leaf but nothing stirred. The spider must have come from the diggers camp. It saddened him to think it might have died of the cold. But perhaps it was just hibernating like the little bee queen in her urn. Or maybe this was an egg sac.

Bily dropped back to the ground and continued walking behind the wagon, thinking how much easier it had been not to brood in the cottage. There had always been so much to do.

If there was not cleaning and cooking and tending to his garden, there had been spinning and weaving and pots to be fired or coloured, or he had experimented with dye colours.

How he missed the purposefulness of his old life. Travelling, you saw many new and interesting things, and everything you saw roused questions. That must be why Zluty was always asking questions. He had got in the habit of it during his foraging journeys, and thinking always seemed to lead to more questions.

Just the night before, Zluty had asked Flugal

to tell him again how the Makers had gone from using the sky crack as a place to put things they did not want, to risking injury or death to creatures and damage to machines so they could explore it.

'What suddenly made them so interested in what was on the other side of the sky crack?' Zluty had asked.

Flugal answered that the Makers could not endure mysteries. They wanted to know everything. Which made them sound rather like Zluty, Bily suddenly thought.

As to the diggers and Cloud Monster and all the others sent through the sky crack, perhaps the Makers regarded them less as living servants than as machines and devices to be used as they wished. When the diggers smashed the stone storm machine that they had assembled and repaired, perhaps the Makers simply decided they were faulty machines and so sent the Monks to fix them. Before submitting them to the Makers machine, the Monks had fitted the diggers with metal on the *outside* of their heads which would bond it to the metal *inside* their heads and make them obedient. Perhaps the Makers saw that as repairing the diggers.

Bily wondered if he was right about the diggers being able to defy their masters because they had been angry. It had only just occurred to him as he said it to the Monster. But the Monster *had* defied its binding out of fear of the *arosh*. And the magnificent Cloud Monster he had met on top of the mountain when he had gone to find Zluty had rebelled against the Makers in rage and anguish after its mate died coming through the sky crack.

The more Bily thought about it, the more it made sense that strong emotions like anger and fear would muddle the Makers metal. Because no matter what the Makers thought, the Monster and the diggers and the Cloud Monster were not machines.

Something cold tapped his nose lightly and he realised that cold fluffs were beginning to fall again. They were big and soft and wet and melted quickly on the ground and on his fur, the wetness seeping through to his skin.

Redwing returned, swooping down to perch on the rim at the back of the wagon. There were little droplets of rain on her feathers, and she was shivering.

'Perch inside next to the Monster if you are cold,' Bily urged.

The bird blinked at him with her dark, shiny eyes and he saw she had not taken in his words, though he had said them with his mind, as well as aloud. The storm of longing to fly West filled her mind, left no room for anything else. He was about to call out to Zluty to stop so he could get up and move her into the wagon, when the Monster looked at Redwing and gave a soft piercing yowl. The red bird looked into its yellow, gleaming eyes as if mesmerised, then she fluttered down from the rim of the wagon.

When Bily climbed up to look inside, he saw that the Monster's tail snaked around the red bird to form a soft, dark nest. As he watched, Redwing fluffed her feathers in cosy contentment and closed her eyes.

Walking in the wake of the wagon again, Bily held the picture of them cuddled together in his mind, blinking his eyes against the falling slush. The mountains were now no more than a dark smudge and, as he plodded along, head down, Bily's thoughts slipped to another memory, this one, of trudging across the white, windswept plateau atop the mountains, where he had encountered the Cloud Monster.

He had been lost, the air filled with flying cold fluffs that seemed to have got inside his head, making it hard to think. The wind had gusted so strongly that the cold fluffs stung his bare face and hands like a hoard of angry bees. He had been walking with his head bowed to protect his cheeks, until something made him look up, and there had been the Cloud Monster looming up like a piece of the storm come to life.

Bily was glad to find that he had such a clear, striking picture of that moment stored in his mind. The first chance he got, he must use a bit of the precious paper the diggers had given him to scratch out a picture of the Cloud Monster, using the nubs of the charcoal he saved from the fire. What he wanted most was to weave it into a great wall rug that could hang in their new cottage. He could imagine just how it would look – the Cloud Monster rising up against a dark purple and grey sky, its icy eyes ablaze, the white cold fluffs flying at its back like a cloak.

He could do a scratching of the Monster and Redwing, too. He might even colour it using some of the stoppered pots of colour the diggers had given him. That must wait until they reached the Vale of Bellflowers and built a new cottage, but the thought warmed Bily as cold fluffs continued to fall and he trudged on alongside the wagon.

4

The wet cold fluffs turned into a heavy rain. They pressed on even though it drenched their thickened pelts and turned the ground to black slush, until a wheel became wedged between two stones. By the time they got it free they were all dripping wet and exhausted.

'We must stop,' Bily shouted to Zluty over the rain noise. 'If we can light a fire under the canopy, we can dry our pelts.'

Zluty did not want to stop and waste what remained of the short day, nor did he want to waste firenuts to dry out pelts that would dry of their own accord once the rain stopped.

'Walking will warm us, but we could have a bite of something to eat before we go on,' he conceded.

When they had all clambered into the wagon, Bily shouted to be heard over the rain drumming on the canopy. 'We can't *see* where we are going in this. That's why the wheel got stuck.'

It was true. The rain had been falling so hard that Zluty had to walk with his head down or be blinded, and it was a dark day with the thick grey clouds overhead. Still, he did not want to stop. He looked at Flugal. 'Do you think we should go on?'

Instead of agreeing, Flugal went to consult the other diggers. But it was Semmel who brought their answer. 'We think stopping and resting and eating is best, because rain will stopping soon and we can still reach the flyway before the endfulness of day.'

Zluty had no choice but to surrender, because having asked the diggers' opinion it would be rude to ignore it.

'I can make a proper hot supper,' Bily said and opened out the awnings on the lee side of the wagon.

Zluty scraped a shallow firepit, thinking how lucky it was they had the miraculous moss balls with their fiery core, for he needed only a few embers and some firenuts to conjure a warm blaze. They were all soon clustered around the fire under the dripping edges of the awning, their fur beginning to steam. Bily carried a pot out of the wagon upon which floated tiny dried onions and mushrooms, and soon it was bubbling away over the fire. Zluty's mouth watered as he smelled the rich savoury scent of the rare black mushroom he had found in his last visit to the Northern Forest.

Bily's fur had dried, and while the food cooked he got out his brush. But before he could use it, Semmel took it from him.

'I will do the brushing of the fluffiness,' she said.

Bily said uncertainly, 'That would be lovely.'

Zluty watched, not sure why it made him smile to see Bily suffering his fur to be brushed by Semmel, and then several other diggers who brought out their own little combs and came to help. The brushing went on for some time, and if Bily had not suddenly said very firmly but politely that the food was ready, Zluty felt the diggers would have gone on brushing him dreamily deep into the night.

As Bily began to serve up bowls of food, a speckled digger reached out shyly to touch his tail. 'You are very softy,' she said admiringly, patting Bily's tail, which really had fluffed up rather splendidly.

'Thank you,' Bily muttered, his cheeks as red as the flames.

Soon they were all eating their stew sitting in a row under the awning, gazing out at the thunderous curtain of rain that hid the world from them.

'It would be very horrible to be out in that,' Bily said.

Zluty had to agree, and he did feel better for the rest and a hot meal. The rain had washed the mud out of his fur and so he used Bily's brush to tidy himself while several of the diggers upturned their empty bowls and began to tap out a little rain beat. Zluty laid down the brush and listened in delight.

'Join, *Zchloo-tee*!' invited one of the diggers, offering him his reed pipe.

Zluty took it but laid it aside and upturned his bowl. He listened carefully for a while, then he took a firenut in each hand and began to hammer out a rhythm of his own, feet slapping on the wet ground, every now and then rapping on the staff. The diggers squeaked in delight and Zluty grinned, hearing them clap the lighter patter of the digger paws into the rain and the sound of his feet.

Bily was packing away the cooking things when suddenly he burst out laughing. Startled, Zluty and the diggers stopped tapping and turned to look at him. In the silence, Zluty understood. They had been so busy playing the sound of the rain that they had not noticed that it had ceased. Now, there

was just the crackle of the fire and water dripping from the awning.

'We must going on,' Flugal said regretfully.

It did not take them long to roll up the ground sheets they had been sitting on and lower the sodden awning. Semmel scraped the few glowing embers from the fire back into the firemoss ball and closed it, while Bily collected several blackened nubs of firenuts in a pot he hung from the side of the wagon.

As they set off again, Zluty was pleased to see that it was not so dark now that the rain had stopped. The greyish light told him there was at least an hour of day left.

The sound of wings made them all turn to see Redwing launch herself into the air. Zluty watched her fly up and angle North. He wondered if she sensed the nearness of the flyway and would go through it at once when she came to it, without saying goodbye. He could not blame her for obeying the call to fly West, but Bily would be terribly hurt.

Flugal had told them that before the first stone storm, flocks of red-winged birds had always flown West on the eve of Winter. Cloud after fiery cloud of them had risen until there had been so many of them flying over the mountains that they had formed a great red bridge spanning the sky from East to West. Flugal had not seen the splendid sight he described, but the telling was sung often and he had a very clear picture of it in his mind, which he had been able to show Zluty and Bily. The red-winged birds had gone West seeking a warm place to lay their eggs and hatch their younglings. When Spring came, they had returned East.

This story had made Bily sad, for the great flocks of red birds had perished and Redwing was the last of her kind. There would be no mate or younglings for her in the West.

Zluty noticed Semmel gazing after the red bird, too, sorrow and regret in her bright eyes. He knew the diggers blamed themselves for the tragic destruction of Redwing's kind, because they had built the Makers stone storm machine from parts sent through the sky crack. Yet all of that had happened long before Semmel was born, and those early diggers had not known what the machine they were making would do. When they did understand, they had broken the machine.

Semmel looked at him questioningly.

'I was wondering how close we are to the flyway,' said Zluty.

'We will reach it soonly,' the she digger said calmly.

Flugal suddenly pointed up with a *Ra!* of delight, and Zluty saw that Redwing had turned back and was overhead, coiling and soaring in the air high above them. Bily looked relieved, but Zluty wondered if Redwing was staying close because she knew that all too soon she would leave them.

Then Bily caught his arm and pointed to the mountains.

Zluty saw a great hole high up in the wet, stony slope of the nearest mountain. It was visible only because a dazzling beam of light flowed from it, turning the mist clinging to the side of the mountain a golden gauze. It was as if a stream of bright Summer daylight shone into the Winter twilight.

'Sunlight from the West,' Semmel murmured. 'That is the flyway.'

Redwing flew low and began to sing them a farewell, but Bily interrupted to beg her to land and let him prepare her some food before she left. Zluty felt the strength of Redwing's urgency to be gone, yet her love for Bily was very strong, too. She gave one piercing cry before settling, and then she stood patiently, allowing the diggers to reverently groom and smooth her ruffled feathers, while Bily mixed her favourite seeds and some honey water.

Zluty took out his pipe and played a tune. He did not want to play a mournful tune for the occasion was sad enough. Instead, he tried to think how exciting it would be for Redwing to enter the mysterious flyway and soar into sunlight and the warmth. If the weather truly was hot on the other side of the mountains, it would be like flying from Winter to Summer, as well as from night into day. His tune drew on all of these thoughts, but it also caught up Redwing's longing to fly into the West. It was a song of yearning that told of Bily singing out to him to come for supper, or to see a new dye he had discovered, or a new rug he had begun. He piped the diggers in their burrows, calling one another to eat. He played the baby birds in their nests, cheeping to their mothers to come and feed them.

Redwing cocked her head and watched him intently, occasionally making a soft cooing noise. The diggers joined in, clapping their paws softly together at the chorus to make a sound like the beat of a bird's wings.

Bily brought a bowl and set it before Redwing. She began at once to peck at the seeds. Zluty was startled to see that some of them had come from the precious store of seeds Bily had scavenged from the drowned cellar of their cottage. They were all that remained of his garden. He had dried them out for when he might have a garden again, yet he had sacrificed some of them to Redwing.

When the bird had finished, she looked at Bily and spread one wing to enfold him and gather him close. He laid his head against her breast sadly and Zluty knew he was listening to the soft thud of

Redwing's heart. He had told Zluty that this was one of his favourite sounds in all the world.

He heard Bily whisper to Redwing that he loved her and already longed for the day when they were together again. Finally, unable to resist the calling any longer, Redwing freed herself, shook her plumage out and sang a farewell.

For once, the words in her mind were so strong that even Zluty heard them clearly. She was telling Bily that she loved him, and would carry him to the West in her heart. Then, to his surprise, she reached across to tap Zluty's cheek tenderly with her beak and bid him farewell, too.

'Guard Bily,' she sent the thought softly, gravely, just for him, then she flapped up to the side of the wagon where the Monster was watching them with its yellow eyes. It looked at the bird and, though he could hear nothing, Zluty had the feeling they were talking to one another.

At length, Redwing turned to the diggers who had gathered reverently into a little group by the side of the wagon, their heads raised so they could look at her. She sang a sweet, high note of farewell wound up with forgiveness to them, then she leapt into the air. Opening her lovely wings to their fullest extent she beat them powerfully, once, twice, thrice, rising higher and higher above them, and the diggers clapped their soft wingbeat song as she glided over them and away towards the mountains.

Zluty watched her soar across the stony face of the mountain to the hole where the golden light flowed through. Without hesitation, she angled her wings and soared into the flyway. For a moment her red plumage blazed like fire, and then she was gone.

'Oh,' Bily cried, as if he had cut himself.

'She flies as her heart desires,' said the Monster in its dark soft tone, its eyes fixed on the flyway.

Zluty heard the clear note of envy in its voice. He took his brother's hand and patted it. 'I am sure it is not forever,' he told Bily gently. 'Now, we must set up camp and get some sleep. I won't make another fire for we don't need to eat again tonight, but perhaps we ought to have a farewell breakfast tomorrow. The diggers who are to return to their settlement will want to leave early.'

As Zluty had guessed, his words distracted his brother from his immediate grief and Bily announced that he would prepare everything for the feast before he slept.

When Zluty offered to help, Bily refused in a muffled voice. Seeing that he needed to be alone to grieve for a bit, Zluty went to check on the bee urn carefully stowed in the wagon. He wanted to make sure no water had leaked into the urn or into anything else that might be damaged by it. He was relieved to find that nothing had been spoiled or made more than slightly damp. Bily had told him the awning had been treated with some potion that resisted water, and Zluty reminded himself to find out how it was made before they parted from the diggers, so that he could make more when it wore off.

He went to help the diggers untie all the metal pieces of the devices they were taking back to the settlement. He was dismayed to see how many there were. Two pieces were so big that it would take three diggers to carry one.

'They can't manage all of this,' he said to Flugal. 'We had better make a pile of them here and they can come back to collect them.'

But Flugal said the diggers were determined to take all of their treasures back to the settlement.

'Well,' said Zluty, studying the pile, 'we could tie everything onto the two big pieces and fix it so the diggers can pull them like the wagon. We can't make wheels, so when there are no coldwhites like now, they must carry them.'

This was such a clever idea that the diggers agreed at once, and Flugal set about hammering the bigger bits into shapes that would enable them to be pulled along in the snow.

'They are very odd looking,' Bily said doubtfully, coming to see how they were doing.

'They don't have to look nice,' Zluty told him firmly. 'They only have to work.'

Zluty helped Flugal with the sleds as the dull afternoon light faded. There was no wind and Zluty hoped it would stay that way, for it had got a good deal colder now. His eyes sought out the flyway where a soft haze of brightness still shone, and he thought of Redwing, flying on and on into the dying light.

5

Bily listened to the diggers chattering as
some of them helped Semmel bundle up
the supplies they would tie to the sleds.
He was making the batter for the pancakes he
would cook in the morning, but most of his mind
was taken up with grieving for Redwing.

He was ashamed of it because the Monster was
right. Redwing was going where she had been longing to go, and he had no right to be sad. But he
wept a good many quiet tears into the big pot of
pancake batter he was mixing, carefully avoiding
looking at the Monster, whose golden gaze rested

on him from time to time.

Bily's eyes were drawn again and again to the flyway, where gradually the haze of light streaming from the opening had darkened from gold to orange to dusky red.

Finally, the opening was lost in the hulking darkness of the mountains and he heaved a sigh. He had secretly hoped that Redwing might discover the pull of her love for him was stronger than her desire to fly into the mysterious West. But she had not returned. She would not return. How long would it take her to fly through a mountain? he wondered.

Unable to bear thinking of her all alone in the stony heart of the mountains with no fire to warm her, no one to cuddle to her, Bily reminded himself that Redwing did not have to trudge through the snow but flew on swift, wide wings with a strong wind from the East behind her.

He tried to imagine her landing somewhere in the Velvet City, but it was too hard to imagine a place he had never seen. The diggers had never seen it either, and the Monster had said only that it was hot and that there were many Listeners living there in complex many-levelled cottages made from stone. Bily found it difficult to imagine many cottages all pressed close to one another, let alone cottages on top of one another. He had only ever known the cottage where he and Zluty had lived.

The Monster said softly, 'You smell of memories.'

Bily fancied there was disapproval in its voice. He said, 'I was thinking of the things you told me about the Velvet City when we first met.'

The Monster's eyes glimmered with brief rare humour. 'You smelled of fear then, but still you tended my wounds. Is that how you came to know Redwing? You healed her?'

It hurt Bily so much to hear Redwing's name, that for a moment he could not breathe.

'I heard her singing,' he managed to say, the memory of that first song so sweet and dear. 'Zluty was away in the Northern Forest and there was a grass fire. I had not seen it coming but I smelled it. I was trying to wet the garden so that the sparks would not catch, when I heard Redwing. I could not see her for the smoke. I thought I was imagining it, but she kept singing. I found her in a little thicket in the grass just before the fire burned it.'

'Where did she come from before that?' the Monster asked.

'She could not say. She was only a youngling. She could not even have flown there because she had no feathers, only a bit of fluff on her head. The rest of her was pink and bare. But there was a terrible storm before the fire came. It must have blown Redwing before it. She has no memory of what was before that, so maybe she was inside an egg.'

'Storms do have a habit of bringing the world to your door, Bily,' the Monster said. 'Perhaps Redwing came from the same place as the fire.'

Bily opened his mouth to say that was impossible because the fire had been lit by burning talons of sky fire, but Semmel suddenly gave a muffled cry of triumph. She had found the sack of dried berries she had decided would go well with pancakes. Bringing them to Bily, she explained that the glossy black berries grew on the stony plain in small pockets of good earth, and were difficult to find. She gave him one to taste. The berry had an unusual tart sweetness, and after a moment of thought he bid her put some of them in a big bowl of water to soak.

The she digger looked surprised and interested as she went to unstopper one of the water urns. She had to lean so far into it with the dipper that she almost overbalanced, reminding Bily the water in it was getting low and he should ask Zluty to fill them from the stream running along the feet of the mountains before they moved on.

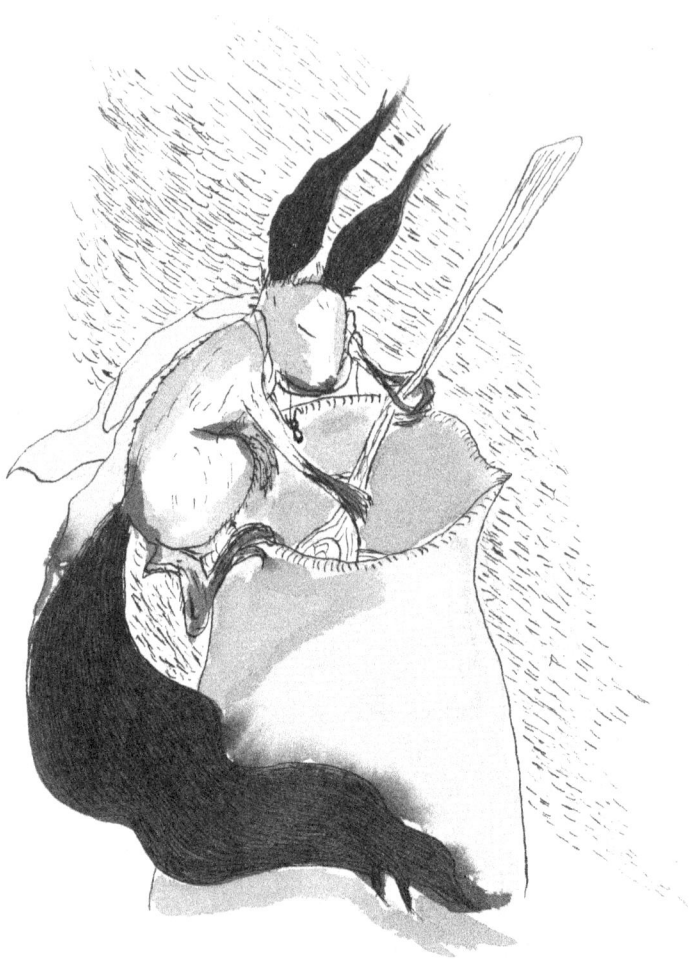

'Tonight will be very mistful,' Semmel murmured as she plucked the hard little stems from the dried berries and put them into a bowl half filled with water. When she had finished, Bily set it atop a shelf. He looked out through the awning to see that the sky was devoid of stars. The mountains had been swallowed up by the dark night, and when his eyes dropped to the ground, a thick white mist was seeping from the earth just as Semmel had predicted. Zluty and the diggers, sitting a little way off, looked as if they were on a little island surrounded by a vaporous sea of white.

Zluty shouted out to Semmel to fetch him the ball of firemoss, and Bily wondered what had made him change his mind about not having a fire. He shrugged and went back to mixing his batter. When it was as fluffy as he liked, he set it beside the bowl of soaking berries and carefully covered both with a cloth. It was warm inside the wagon with the door closed, and the heat given off by the Monster would make the batter rise slowly during the night.

He set about chopping nuts and beating digger milk into butter. By the time Bily finished preparations and stepped outside, it had got darker and the tide of mist had risen high enough that the wagon was submerged. It was very much colder than it had been, and he guessed this must be why Zluty had changed his mind about the fire. He could just see it through the mist, a brave little node of brightness. As he went closer he saw that Zluty and the diggers were poring over a pile of the diggers' small staffs and a heap of shining skystones that gave off their queer greenish light.

He remembered, then, that Zluty had decided to give one skystone to each of the diggers as a farewell present. Obviously he had decided to attach them to their staffs. He had needed the fire to melt the glue that would hold the skystones in place.

Bily decided to give each digger a feather to attach to their staff as well. He went back into the wagon to get his collection and set it down by the fire. The diggers stroked the feathers in delight, and made their choices solemnly. The diggers had their own tokens and treasures which they also added to their staffs, and when each was complete, Zluty bound its grip, and the digger bore it away to bed, chittering in delight.

Despite his thickening fur, Bily shivered as the fire grew low. There were three diggers yet to have their grips bound. All were wrapped up in their cloaks and yawning. Bily went to fetch his own cloak. He saw that Semmel was already curled into her bedding in the wagon, alongside the Monster. Bily carried Zluty's bedding outside and prepared it. He would sleep in the wagon, but Zluty always slept out if he could.

By the time he returned to the fire, only Flugal remained. But he, too, stood and gestured to them to sleep well before trotting off to join Semmel with his staff.

'All is ready for tomorrow?' Zluty asked Bily, stifling a yawn.

'Of course,' Bily said, trying to sound cheerful.

Zluty gave him a searching look. To avoid talking about Redwing, Bily began to tell him about the Monster's warning to avoid the Velvet City.

Zluty frowned. 'Flugal said we have not yet come halfway in our journey to the end of the mountain range, so it will be a good long while before we need to think about the Velvet City. He said we would know we were halfway to the end of the mountains when we come to the Raincage. He doesn't know what that is, but he says the memory scents will tell us.' He smothered another yawn.

'You should go to bed,' Bily told him. 'I made it up for you.' He pointed.

'You ought to go to bed, too, for Flugal said no watch is necessary here,' Zluty told him.

'I am not sleepy,' Bily told him. 'I will sit by the fire until the embers burn out.'

After Zluty had gone, Bily waited until all the rustlings and murmurings of the others fell silent, and there was only the soft crackle of the fire, then he took out his brush from his pack, shrugged off his cloak and slowly began to brush himself. It was wonderfully soothing to feel the tug of the brush.

The mist about him continued to thicken so that before long he was surrounded by white. It was very eerie. He might have been all alone in the world, but for his little pack and the dying fire. This was how it had been for Zluty whenever he travelled to the Northern Forest, Bily thought, and shivered. Putting his brush back into his pack, he pulled his cloak around his shoulders again and sat gazing into the embers.

He told himself he ought to go to bed. It was so cold now that his breath came out in little puffs of cloud, and the thought of cuddling up to the warm bulk of the Monster was lovely. But he did not get up.

'Soon,' he told himself, gazing into the dying heart of the fire.

Zluty woke to a thick white icy mist pressing lightly on his face. He threw off his blanket and, standing up, took a step out from under the awning. His foot slipped out from under him and he sat down hard in the midst of his bedding. Puzzled, he reached out to touch the ground only to discover it was hard and cold and smooth. The water-soaked earth had frozen solid.

He groped for his staff and used it to help him stay upright as he made his careful way to the wagon door. The sun would soon rise, he reassured himself, and even if they could not see it, the world would brighten and warm and melt the ice underfoot.

He resolved to light a fire and then wake Bily and the diggers, but by the time he was getting a few firenuts from the net, several of the diggers were up and folding their blankets, carrying them into the mist in the direction of the sleds.

'Bring a ball of firemoss down to me and then wake Bily,' he told Semmel when she poked her head over the run of the wagon. He added the digger gesture that meant *please*. She nodded and withdrew.

Kneeling to pile fresh firenuts on top of the ashes of the previous night's fire, Zluty thought of what the Monster had said to Bily about not going into the Velvet City because there were strict rules about comings and goings. It occurred to him that the Monster itself had broken the rules by leaving.

6

Zluty wondered what happened when you broke the rules of the Velvet City. Nothing good, probably, hence the Monster's warning.

Was it just curiosity that made him want to go there? Certainly his curiosity had got him in trouble before. Look what had happened when he left the digger camp because he was curious about the Monks. He had ended up being captured by them, and if not for Bily and the diggers he would have had his head emptied. As it was, he still wore one of the Monks' metal devices on his head. The diggers had tried to remove it after he escaped, but one bit of it went inside him and they had not known how to get it out without hurting him. They had assured him the metal would not give the Makers power over him because he did not have Makers metal *inside* him. It seemed the Makers machine could only bind a creature by linking outside Makers metal to inside Makers metal.

He had got used to the feel of the metal on his head and sometimes he quite forgot about it; other times he would touch his head or brush his fur and feel it and long to be free of it. It had occurred to him that there might be a way to get free of it in the Velvet City, but that was not the only reason, nor indeed the most important reason, he wanted to go there.

The main reason was to learn more about the Makers and their plan because he believed he and Bily would need that knowledge to protect themselves and their friends. If the Monster answered his questions about the Makers, he might not feel the need to go to the Velvet City. But even after all the distance they had travelled together, it had told them very little, and now it was clear there were secrets the Monster did not know about the relationship between its people and the Makers.

'I do not like secrets,' Zluty muttered to himself, startling Semmel who had just emerged from the mist. He helped her break open the ball of firemoss and tip some embers onto the pile of firenuts. They began to smoulder at once.

Semmel looked at him through the smudge of smoke and said softly, 'Some secrets are needful, *Zchloo-tee*. The she fire lizard makes a secret of its nest to protect its babies from the he fire lizard who would eat them if he found the eggs or the younglings.'

Zluty stared at her, but before he could say anything she padded away into the roiling mist in the direction of the sleds. He turned back to the firepit and took a pinch of his fur from the pouch where he kept soft wads of fur from various brushings and other tiny bits and pieces that would catch fire easily. He dropped the fur onto the smouldering firenuts. There was a bright, satisfying flare of flame as they caught and began to crackle. Staring into the flame, he thought how Bily had always been content for the world to keep its secrets. But Zluty was not like that. Curiosity beat at his mind just like Redwing's longing to fly into the West.

'If Bily can accept the Monster's secretive nature then he must accept my curiosity,' Zluty muttered. 'It is not as if curiosity is badness.'

His curiosity *had* got him into trouble, but it had also led to important discoveries and useful knowledge. Yet the risk must be worth the gain. The Monster might be able to tell him enough for him to decide, if it would speak. It had woken now and seemed alert, and maybe he could convince it to tell him more about the Velvet City.

The trouble was, Zluty did not completely trust the Monster, even after all they had endured together. It was a Listener and its people served the Makers and worked with the Monks, who served them too, and kept diggers as slaves. The Monster had warned Bily that they should not go to the Velvet City, presumably because it did not want them to come to harm. But Zluty felt in his heart and bones that their ignorance of the Makers and their plan might very well be the most dangerous thing of all.

The Makers had shown themselves to be powerful and destructive. They used other creatures mercilessly, sending them through the sky crack to do their bidding knowing they might be damaged or killed. They had not minded what they destroyed when they sent the stone storm machine. In fact, *that had been their purpose in sending it*. They had sent the Monks to capture rebel diggers and empty their heads out, even though this rendered them unfit for anything but the simplest tasks, so they must also be vengeful.

Zluty sighed and climbed into the wagon.

Bily was almost invisible because the Monster had curled right around him, their pale pelts blending into one another. It took Zluty a moment to see that Bily was sleeping between the Monster's paws, its long dangerous claws unsheathed across his chest. That didn't frighten Zluty. No matter what the Monster thought of the rest of them, Zluty knew that it would do nothing to hurt Bily. Which must be why it had warned them away from the Velvet City.

Zluty leaned over Bily and was startled when his brother opened his eyes and said in a scratchy, unhappy voice, 'I don't understand what I am to do.'

'Hush, you are dreaming,' Zluty told him.

But Bily said fretfully, 'No! The voice . . . The egg . . . It keeps telling me there is something I must do but I don't understand what . . .' His eyes fell closed again.

Zluty stared at his brother in uneasy wonderment. Had he really dreamed of the egg voice too? His own first memory was of that voice, urging him to find food and water on the plain, and later, telling him how to make the egg into a shelter. When they had grown and the egg shelter had got too small, it had instructed him to build a proper cottage. The voice had grown fainter after that, as if dismantling the egg had weakened it. But when the food from the plain ran out, the voice had spoken again, sending Zluty in search of the Northern Forest, where he could get more food. By the time they had finished the cottage and he had turned a remnant of the egg into a wagon to carry things, the voice had fallen silent.

He heard it now only in rare dreams. The last time had been in a nightmare on his last trip to the Northern Forest. The voice had urged him to hurry home before it was too late. Zluty had obeyed, arriving at the ruined cottage just in time to save Bily and the Monster from being drowned in the flooded cellar. And now Bily was dreaming of the voice.

Zluty patted Bily's cheek insistently.

This time, Bily opened his eyes wide and sat up at once, his expression alert, anxious. 'What is it, Zluty? What is wrong?'

'Hush,' Zluty soothed. 'Nothing is wrong. Only it's nearly dawn and I've made a fire. If you want to cook breakfast for the diggers, you must do it now. They are all up and Flugal says they mean to go as soon as the sun rises.'

Bily nodded and, lifting the Monster's paw, carefully unhooked a claw that had got caught in his thick fur. Edging free of its sleeping embrace, he stood up and began to rummage around in the shelves, muttering softly to himself.

He seemed to have no memory of his nightmare and Zluty thought it better not to ask him about it.

'Can I help?' he asked instead, hiding a smile because Bily was so fluffy now that he really did look quite wild.

Bily lifted the bowl of batter into Zluty's arms, telling him to set it by the fire, and a little delegation of diggers carried off all the cooking things. Bily peeped into the bowl of berries as he picked them up, and saw with satisfaction that they had

absorbed much of the water they had been soaking in and now shone, fat and glossy.

Outside, the air was thick with mist. He could see nothing of the land or the mountains and only a smear of reddish light that must be the fire. As he stepped down, the diggers called out to him to take care because the ground was icy.

Bily found that it was very slippery indeed. He did not like the slipperiness, but the mist, billowing wetly on all sides, made the world beautifully cosy. Since they had begun travelling, he had often felt overwhelmed by how big the world was.

It did not take him long to cook up a pile of fluffy golden-brown pancakes. The diggers had come one by one to sit, and Bily had just cooked the berries into a sticky sweet syrup, when Zluty, Flugal and Semmel emerged from the mist.

'They smell wonderful,' Zluty said.

For a time there was nothing but the sound of eating and the companionable crackle of the fire, and Bily glanced around at his companions with the warm, satisfied, safe feeling he always got when he had made some food and it was being eaten. For a little while, he forgot the strange, worrying nightmares that had made him sleep so restlessly.

'What were you all humming before?' Zluty asked Semmel, helping himself to another pancake.

'We are making a song telling the flight of the *Lastling* through the flyway,' Semmel said. 'It is part of the telling of the journey that the diggers will take back to the clan.'

'We will make a telling song of our own journeying when *we* return,' Flugal said. 'All telling songs overlap for greater truthfulness.'

Bily was thinking how beautiful to think of stories told by overlapping songs, when Zluty said, 'Your potion-maker told us Redwing was a sign. He did not say what she was a sign *of*.'

'The coming of the *Lastling* is a sign that great change is coming,' Flugal said gravely.

'But what will change? Is it good or bad? Is it about the coming of the Makers?'

'Nobody can knowing that,' said Flugal.

Zluty looked frustrated, but Bily thought he had not listened well enough. Zluty thought the digger meant that no one could say when the Makers would come. But Flugal's gestures as he spoke added a layer of meaning that meant no one could say what was good or bad in change, because usually there was good *and* bad in any change.

The mist had brightened and it was time for the diggers to leave. Bily wrapped the rest of the pancakes up for the diggers to take with them, and the digger he thought of as Speckledy accepted them and made a gesture that she wanted to speak. Of course, Speckledy was not really her name because it was not the custom among the diggers to name anyone except blood family and a mate. Speckledy bowed to Bily and delivered a brief but heartfelt speech, thanking him for his pancakes and for his gift of feathers and his soft fluffiness.

All of the other diggers stood and bowed to him very solemnly.

Abashed, Bily bowed back.

Speckledy bowed to Zluty, who had come to stand beside him. She thanked him for his staffs and the shining stones and for his music. The other diggers bowed to him too, and Zluty bowed back, wishing them a swift and safe journey home to their settlement.

'Let's go and watch them leave,' Zluty said to Bily as the diggers set off towards the sleds. They looked very strange now that they were upright, but they were not as awkward looking as Bily had thought they would be.

Zluty, Flugal and Semmel carefully lifted each sled so the diggers who would carry it could get into place under it. Zluty examined the sleds and then shifted some of the packs and staffs.

'Better,' Flugal approved, and hung a lit lantern on each sled, then he shouted 'Ra!'

Semmel shouted 'Ra!', too, and the diggers set off, marching East.

They vanished from sight almost at once, leaving Bily, Zluty, Flugal and Semmel staring into the swirling white mist. For a long moment Bily strained his ears to hear the footfalls of the departing diggers, but then there was only the mist and the silence.

'We ought to go, too,' Zluty said.

Flugal began gathering up tools and bits of rope left over from preparing the sleds and Semmel went to get a thick net she had woven, which she explained they must put around the wheels of the wagon to enable them to turn on the icy ground. Impressed with her forethought and her cleverness, Zluty helped to stretch the nets around the wheels and fasten them in place, while Bily boiled a bit of water on the dying fire to wash the plates.

As he oiled the black pan and slotted it into its place, Bily marvelled at how much room there was in the wagon now that the returning diggers had taken their collection of Maker devices. He had not noticed how many had been gathered as they'd travelled, but now that it was possible to walk around rather than climbing over things, he began to think how everything might be arranged more tidily.

Noticing the Monster was awake, he offered it a pancake he had set aside. It ate without much interest and Bily wondered what Listeners *liked* to eat, for though it was always grateful, the Monster had never eaten anything with much pleasure. It seemed distracted and he wondered if it was muddled again. He did not think it could be sad that most of the diggers had gone, for it had paid little attention to them, and sure enough, it made no comment when Bily said most of the diggers had left. Bily missed them already.

'I do not like saying goodbye,' he told Zluty a little later, as he helped to roll up the sides of the canopy and tie them in place.

'They might visit us someday,' his brother said cheerfully, slamming the little hinged door closed and going to take up the lead towrope. Flugal and Semmel remained inside at Zluty's suggestion, wrapped in their cloaks and seated at the front of the wagon. Bily took up the side rope that enabled the wagon to be steered.

Zluty shouted to him to pull, and Bily obeyed with a last glance in the direction of the mountain beside them where Redwing had flown into the flyway. The mountain was only just visible as a great bulk of shadow rising up beside them in the mist.

7

The ground beyond their makeshift camp was so slippery that Bily fell over almost at once, and could not get to his feet without help.

Semmel produced woven nets for their feet that she had fashioned from the same stuff as the wheel nets, saying they would be able to walk without slipping over in them. Bily pulled on the pair he had been given and tied them at the top, then walked about to test them, but Zluty said he would use his staff to steady himself.

Neither the iciness nor the white mist lessened

as the day wore on, for there was not a breath of wind to stir the air. The stillness made Zluty uneasy. They had been walking a good while before he realised that it was not the stillness that bothered him. He had the feeling something was watching them. He told himself it was silly because the mist that hid everything would hide them from any watcher as well.

When they stopped to rest at midday, they brought the wagon closer to the mountains so he could get water from the stream, and he was able to see some way up the nearest dark slope. Zluty studied the glistening flank of the mountain as he lowered the water urns using the nets and levers set up by the diggers, but he saw no movement.

Telling himself he was imagining things, he rolled the urns to the bank of the stream and poured water into them with a jug. There was a little crust of ice along the edges of the stream, but the fast-running current had kept it from freezing over. The water was so cold that it made his hands ache. By the time he finished, his fingers were white and numb.

He had put the fingers of one hand into his mouth to get the blood flowing when he heard the sound of a boulder crashing down the mountain-side. It smashed into a jutting outcrop part way down the face of the mountain not far from where he stood. A little avalanche of stone and rubble fell, as the boulder bounced up and then fell the rest of the way to the ground, breaking into pieces.

Heart hammering, Zluty hurriedly dragged the heavy urns back from the edge of the stream and rolled them back to the wagon. Then he turned to peer at what he could see of the mountains, wondering what had dislodged the boulder.

'What was that?' Bily came running to ask.

'Just a boulder falling,' Zluty said, turning to smile at his brother. 'Help me get the urns back in place, will you?' he added, more to distract Bily than because help was needed.

Once the urns were secured, Zluty almost mentioned the odd feeling he had of being watched. He wanted to ask if his brother had seen or heard any-thing, but in the end, he held his tongue because he knew it would just make Bily anxious. Instead, he resolved to keep watch that night, no matter what the diggers said.

Bily had set out a cold meal of a few pancakes he had set aside from breakfast. As they ate, Zluty was reminded of all the times he had eaten cold pancakes on foraging trips. By the time they finished, it was cold enough that they were all glad to go on. The short day was already dimming, and Zluty suggested that from the following day they should no longer stop during the short day. The few hours of light were too precious to be wasted resting or eating.

They had not long set off before coldwhites began to fall very thickly and softly. Soon they had to stop to remove the wheel nets, which were beginning to collect great clumps of coldwhites. They were just stowing them away when the wind began to blow. It was only a slight breeze that barely stirred the mist to begin with, but it got more and more forceful, until the flying coldwhites began to sting. They endured this by pulling the hoods of their cloaks close about their faces, but in the end they had to stop when the coldwhites were so thick on the ground that it was hard for the wheels to turn. They would have removed them, but the coldwhites were still too soft for them to turn the wagon into a sled.

'There is still at least an hour of daylight left,' Zluty protested. 'We have come hardly any distance at all since midday.'

'I know, but we are not getting anywhere now and we are exhausting ourselves,' Bily said. 'And what if there is a crack or some obstacle hidden by the melting cold fluffs.' He reached out to pat Zluty's shoulder. 'We can leave before the sun rises tomorrow to make up for stopping early today, and we can go on later because the cold fluffs give off so much light,' he said.

'Windfulness will get worse and coldwhites will fall all night,' Semmel added.

Zluty surrendered. 'All right, but I will take the wheels off now so that we can set off tomorrow without wasting any time.'

'Not goodly, *Zchloo-tee*,' Flugal said regretfully, pointing out that coldwhites could fall all night and still melt on the morrow, in which case they would have to replace the wheels before they could go on. 'Better to waiting, since putting on is being harder than taking off.'

Flugal suddenly spotted a fallen Maker device not far away, half covered in coldwhites, and hurried to examine it.

'Anyone would think those broken machines call him like the West called to Redwing,' Zluty muttered. He had spoken softly because he did not want to remind Bily of Redwing's departure, but Semmel was close by.

'Yes,' she said calmly, watching her mate. 'Living Makers metal calling to Makers metal in Flugal.'

Before Zluty could think what to say to this, Bily cried out to them to help tie all the flaps and awnings shut, since they did not want to sleep in a wagon full of puddles of melting cold fluffs.

'I will make a hot soup for supper,' Bily said.

'We can't have a fire, Bily,' Zluty objected. 'If we put up an awning to stop coldwhites falling into the firepit, the wind is like to blow it down, and even if it doesn't, the wind is blowing the cold-whites sideways so *they* would quench the flames.'

'There is room in the wagon to cook, now that so much has been taken out,' Bily replied tranquilly.

'But . . . Bily, we *can't* light a fire in the wagon,' Zluty spluttered, wondering what had possessed his brother to suggest such a thing. The metal of the egg was strong, but it could be melted by heat. He had learned this watching the diggers make changes made to the wagon using heat as a tool.

'Wait,' Bily said and gave him a jug, bidding him to fill it with water.

Zluty went to take water from one of the urns. He could just see Flugal trying to open up the broken Makers device through the falling coldwhites. Zluty would have gone to help him, but the diggers had rejected him when he had tried, saying the metal would not listen to him. Given what Semmel had just said, he supposed he could not hear because he had no Makers metal in him.

Zluty had just brought the water to Bily when the door opened again and Flugal scrambled in. Triumphantly, he held up a device with wires dangling from it. Zluty was relieved to see how small it was.

Setting the device aside, Semmel helped her mate brush the coldwhites off his tail and ears. Zluty mopped them up, for they were already melting. It was warm inside the wagon because of the heat given off by the Monster. Glancing across at it, he was startled to see it was awake. He knew Bily was worried the soothing potion was wearing off, but he resolved to take advantage of its wakefulness since they had been forced to stop. He tried to think what he wanted most to know about the Velvet City, for if the Monster did answer questions, it seldom answered more than one or two.

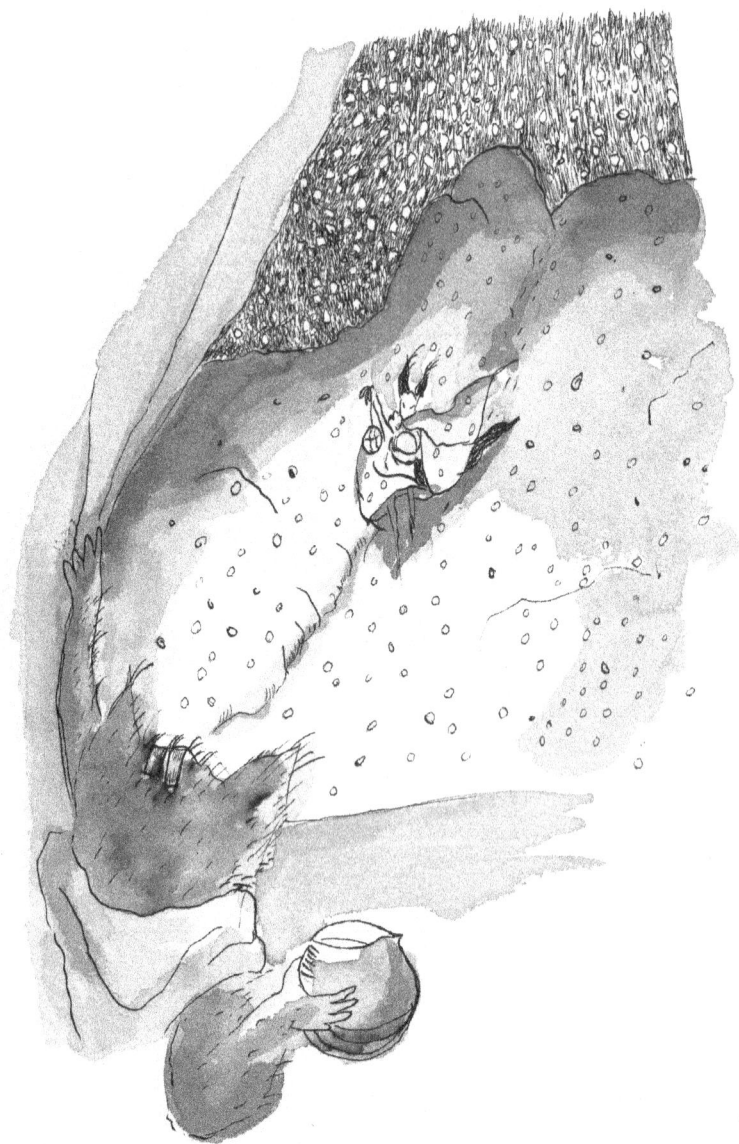

Bily interrupted his thoughts by asking him to help Semmel.

The she digger was struggling with a wide flat metal disc. He went to help and was startled at how heavy it was. In the end, Flugal had to help them lift it carefully onto the frame that Bily had set up. They moved the disc around until it was balanced and then Bily pushed little clips into place, fixing the disc to its base. It looked rather like the cottage table, except it was low and round and curved up at the outer edge.

Bily mounded some firenuts on it and bade Zluty get the firemoss ball and set them alight. Once the firenuts were smouldering, he dropped a little wad of fluff onto them, and even as the fire flared to life, he deftly dropped a bowl of metal mesh over it.

Bily set a pot atop the mesh bowl, and Zluty realised that it must be made of the same special metal as the metal disc, else it would have melted.

Bily dropped a knob of digger butter into the pot and, as he cut and chopped a tuber and some mushrooms and then poured in water from the jug, Semmel bustled to and fro around him, sniffing the broth and adding this or that pinch of herb or powder, occasionally consulting with Bily.

The she digger was humming and Zluty thought he recognised the telling song he had heard the departed diggers singing, though it was hard to be sure over the wind, which had begun to howl and moan.

Flugal began examining the device he had brought back, and, watching him, Zluty realised the queer apprehension that someone or something was watching them, which had haunted him all day, had finally gone. It was absurd to think any creature would be lurking out in such weather, spying on them!

He suddenly felt very weary. It was one thing to work hard and walk far, but worrying was more tiring than days of tramping over the plain.

As the soup bubbled away, its delicious, complicated, savoury smell filled the air, making it even warmer inside the wagon. Zluty lay back against the bale of sweetgrass Bily had insisted on bringing so he could stuff their mattresses in the new cottage. The smell of it reminded him of harvesting the sweetgrass. He relaxed but he did not want to sleep. He no longer felt the need to keep watch, but he was looking forward to being awake after

all of the others slept. A part of him missed the
solitude of the days on the plain, when he had gone
off to forage alone. He loved Bily, and he enjoyed
the company of the diggers, their busy, endless
interesting chatter. But sometimes he wanted a bit
of time alone with his thoughts.

To keep himself awake, Zluty got out his little
reed pipe. It was cold to the touch, and when he
began to play, the music he got from it was thin,
but gradually it warmed. He thought for a moment,

then played a tune of harvesting the coldwhites Bily later spun into thread. The two diggers leaned together to listen as he went on to play Bily in the garden with the little birds hopping around him. At length they joined in, clapping out the sound of the birds, and when he played of the flowers breaking out of their seeds, showing their faces to the sun and drinking in the rain, they clapped out the rain song they had made days before.

They made music until the food was ready and Bily asked Zluty to fetch a loaf of bread to break into pieces in the soup bowls. The bread was hard and dry but it would soften and thicken the broth. When he had finished, Bily poured soup into the bowls and Zluty passed them to Flugal and Semmel.

Spooning up his own food, Zluty watched as Bily held a bowl of the broth he had cooled for the Monster to lap at. Only when it had finished, did Bily sit down and eat his own soup. When they had all finished and the dishes were done and put away, Bily rose to put out the fire, now only a pile of glowing ashes, but Semmel stopped him. When he stepped back, she used a spoon to remove the hot mesh bowl and then dropped a pinch of dust from a small pouch onto the ashes.

A beautiful green spiral of smoke rose up and a sweet, lovely scent filled the air.

'What is it?' Bily asked in delight.

'It is memory dust,' said Semmel. 'For keeping memories.'

Her voice was dreamy, and to Zluty's and Bily's startled delight, the she digger began to dance, moving her paws in a graceful swooping motion that reminded Zluty of Bily sewing a rug, and then of Redwing, swooping in a high wind. The greenish smoke coiled up for a long time as Semmel danced, pushing and swirling her paws through it so that it coiled and floated all through the wagon. She was humming a song very softly, adding to it as she went over and over it.

'She is dancing the memories into the smoke,' Flugal said, watching his mate with shining eyes, the bit of the metal device for the moment forgotten in his lap. He pointed to the mound of ashes from which the greenish smoke still rose. 'Later she will harvest the ash.'

Semmel danced on and on and Zluty watched until his eyes began to droop.

Outside, the wind howled and coldwhites fell and fell.

8

Zluty woke with a start, and wondered what had woken him. The wind was howling and coldwhites were slapping against the awning, but they were the same sounds he had been listening to before he fell asleep. Then he remembered that he had meant to stay awake for a time after the others slept.

He sat up and looked around. It was very dark but there was a lantern powered by a Makers device hung from the awning frame at the front of the wagon. By its soft light, he saw that everyone was asleep – Semmel and Flugal curled together,

Bily lying on his bedding by the Monster. The fire table was still standing and there was a trace of the sweet scent of the greenish smoke in the air.

Zluty leaned back against the bale of sweetgrass with a sigh, and turned his thoughts to the Makers as he did in every quiet moment. He was annoyed with himself because despite being determined to question the Monster about the Makers while they were stopped and it was awake, he had fallen asleep. Now he was awake and the Monster was asleep.

Zluty sighed in frustration.

He had asked Flugal as they walked together the day before why the Makers wanted to widen the sky crack and come through. The he digger had told him the Makers needed more space for making because they had used it all up on the other side of the sky crack. Zluty had the cheering thought that, being small, he and Bily might be able to escape their attention, but then remembered the diggers were even smaller than he and Bily, and still the Makers had sent the Monks to capture them and empty their heads!

Outside, the wind got stronger and the wagon began to rock. The movement made the lantern swing to and fro and Zluty noticed that the shadows on the Monster's face shifted as the light did. One moment it appeared sad, and the next, sly and full of malice.

The Monster stirred and one paw twitched. Zluty wished he had the power to look into its dreams.

As if it felt the weight of his thoughts, the Monster stirred again and curled itself around Bily before settling. The sight reassured Zluty, for no matter what secrets it held, the sombre beast truly loved his brother, and would never do anything to bring him to harm. The trouble was, once the Monster was back in the Velvet City and under the control of the Makers machines, it might forget how it felt about Bily and tell its people about them. Then it was likely the Listeners would tell the Makers what they had learned.

A frightening thought occurred to Zluty.

The Monks had seen Bily riding on the back of the Cloud Monster to rescue Zluty. If they had told their masters about that, and the Listeners then told the Makers about them, they might become interested in Bily and him, just as they had become interested in the sky crack, and look where that had led.

Bily gave a moan and thrashed about in his sleep, and Zluty realised he was having another nightmare. He got up and went over to soothe him, only to see that his own travelling pack was humped up awkwardly under Bily's head. Zluty was puzzled because he distinctly remembered pushing the pack into one of the lower niches when they had been readying the wagon in the digger settlement. The diggers must have pulled it out when they were collecting their devices to take back to the settlement.

Carefully, Zluty eased the pack out from under Bily and carried it back to the bale of sweetgrass. He opened the pack and took out the little metal egg he had found in the Northern Forest. It was small and nearly weightless but very hard. No wonder Bily had been sleeping restlessly. He held it up, and the soft lantern light caught the raised pattern around its seal. They were very like the markings on the broken seal of the enormous metal egg he had also found in a burned place in the Northern Forest. Given all he had learned, he thought the bones of the immense, long-dead beast inside it had probably been those of another creature sent through the sky crack by the Makers that had not survived its journey.

The plains' diggers had been drawn to the small egg, and Zluty supposed now that was because the metal of whatever was in it had called to their metal, just as Makers devices called to Flugal. The Monks had been dismayed when they'd discovered the metal egg on Zluty while he was their captive, because they thought it was a stolen message egg, and feared to be blamed by the Makers for carelessness.

Then one sly Monk had suggested that if they did not open the egg, and emptied Zluty's mind so that he forgot where he found it, the Listeners would be blamed for its loss and punished instead of the Monks, since message eggs came from the Velvet City.

The Monster had later said that it was not a message egg. Zluty shook it, wondering what was inside it. To begin with he and Bily had thought that some small creature might hatch out of it, though neither of them had been able to sense life in it. Later they tried and failed to open it. In the end, they kept it because Bily said it was beautiful and must have a place of honour in their new cottage. Zluty suspected Bily secretly hoped that one day something marvellous would hatch out of it.

For him, the egg was a reminder of the Northern Forest. Despite the danger, and the distance from their old cottage, Zluty had loved his journeys there. He had wanted them to go and live there after their cottage was destroyed by the stone storm, but the Monster had insisted they would perish, devoured by giant beasts that took refuge there in the Winter. Zluty had been unable to argue because he had never been there in the Winter. He had reluctantly agreed to go West, because the Monster's description of a soft green land had echoed the vision a bee queen had of them living peacefully in the Vale of Bellflowers.

He wondered whether the bee queen's foreseeing would change if the Makers came.

Everything came back to the Makers, thought Zluty, even though he and Bily were not part of their plan. The diggers even used gestures with their names that meant *the unplanned*. Yet they had saved the life of the Monster, who *was* part of the plan, and Zluty had been captured by the Monks because of the Makers plan, and now they were travelling with diggers who had rebelled against the plan.

Zluty realised he was absentmindedly running a finger along the smooth metal device clasped to his head. He made himself stop and put the metal egg back in his pack and pushed it into an empty niche alongside his bedding. Then he yawned and lay down, all at once weary with thinking about questions that had no answers.

Bily stretched and sat up, only to find the Monster sitting up for the first time since they had left the digger settlement. Its eyes blazed yellow and the fluffs on each ear tip were as stiff as its whiskers.

'What is the matter?' Bily whispered, seeing that everyone else was still asleep.

'I can smell something,' it said. It sounded alert but not alarmed.

'What?' Bily asked.

'I do not know,' said the Monster, and after a little while it lay down again and closed its eyes.

Bily frowned, wondering if the Monster might be getting feverish again, imagining things. Then he realised that it was quiet.

The wind had stopped!

He climbed over the diggers and pulled himself eagerly up onto the rim of the wagon. He unfastened a section of the awning and put his head out.

9

The air was frigid and Bily's breath came out in little clouds. Cold fluffs had ceased to fall but there were no stars, which meant clouds still lay overhead. His senses told him it was very near dawn.

Dropping his gaze, he gasped to see the ground was now covered completely in a thick blanket of white that gave off a soft radiance.

He climbed out of the awning and dropped to the ground. He sank up to his knees in the cold fluffs, but he did not feel the stone underneath his feet, which meant a layer had settled and firmed under the powdery fresh-fallen cold fluffs. With luck it would support the weight of the wagon, in which case the wheels could be removed to turn it into a sled. That would please Zluty, because it would mean they could travel more quickly.

Getting the wheels off would be no small task, however, for the cold fluffs were mounded over the wheels. He was facing the East, and he saw a brightening along the seam of the horizon that confirmed it was almost dawn. Although the wind had dropped almost to nothing, there were still occasional gusts that scooped up cold fluffs and whirled them away. He turned to follow one white dervish to the South when, from the corner of his eye, he caught the movement of something large and dark across the face of the mountains.

Heart banging in his chest, he turned to look, but there was nothing. Frowning, he studied the place where he had seen the movement, but there was nothing but the bulky darkness of the mountains. He thought of the mirages of the desert, where the shimmering heat and the veils of sand had tricked their eyes into seeing things that were not real. Perhaps the cold and the wind wove mirages here, too.

He set off away from the wagon, pushing his way through the cold fluffs. He wanted to feel himself all alone in the vast cold glowing whiteness. There was something lonely and yet thrilling about it. He walked for a little, then stopped, exalting in the cold white world, but when he turned to make his way back to the wagon, he gave a cry of delight. Almost all the awnings on the wagon were closed and lantern light shone through the cloth making it glow like a warm ember. Where he had left the awning open, a slash of warmer yellow light reached out towards him, seeming to offer a pathway back.

Bily tried to fix a picture of it in his mind, so that one day, when they lived in their new cottage, he could create new plates and cups and colour them with images of this strange world. On just one he would paint the glowing wagon.

It was only as he made his way back, that he noticed the cold fluffs on the other side of the wagon were a good deal higher than on the side where he had jumped down. Semmel looked out from under the awning and Bily signalled her to throw down the shovel. He carried it to the drift of cold fluffs against the other side of the wagon and began to dig into it so that he could get to the

net sack of firenuts. He was determined to make porridge for breakfast, even if it did delay them. It would fill them up so they could go the whole day without stopping, as Zluty wanted.

Zluty opened his eyes to daylight and silence, only to discover he was alone in the wagon but for the sleeping Monster.

'Someone ought to have woken me,' he muttered crossly.

Seeing the awning open on the side opposite the wagon door, he was puzzled, but he clambered over bundles and bedding to look out. The coldwhites had stopped falling and the ground was covered in a marvellous blanket of pure white that stretched away under the clouded sky to lap up against the edge of the mountains. There were patches of snow here and there on the dark slopes, but the tops of the mountains were entirely capped in coldwhites, so that it was hard to see where their peaks ended and the sky began.

There was no sign of the others, but Zluty could see Bily's footprints and the pawprints of the diggers disappearing around the wagon. Wondering again why the others had not used the door, he went to unlatch it. The door would not budge.

He returned to the other side of the wagon, climbed onto the rim and jumped down to follow the footprints around to the other side. He saw at once why they had not used the door. It was buried under a great drift of coldwhites that had built up on that side of the wagon. A hole had been dug into it, and when Zluty peered into it he saw the net of firenuts.

That made him realise he could smell smoke. He went further round the wagon and found a flat place that had been stamped down around the heavy metal top of the firetable, which lay flat on the ground. A small crackling fire blazed on it, under the mesh bowl, and a pot of porridge sat on it, bubbling sluggishly.

There was no sign of Bily or the diggers.

Zluty looked around and saw a furrow in the blanket of coldwhites, running East. Following it with his eyes, he saw something sticking up from the whiteness a good way off. Flugal must have found another Makers device, he thought. That explained why Bily had not woken him. Flugal would not leave until he had dug up the device that called to him.

Zluty took the shovel and began to dig out the wheels. By the time Bily returned, he had got two free. He was about to ask how long Flugal would be when he saw Bily's face, suffused with wonder.

'What is it?' he asked.

'It was *singing*,' Bily said.

Zluty stared at him. 'What was singing?'

'The machine Flugal found,' Bily said, his eyes very wide. 'It is the biggest one I have ever seen. Flugal says one piece inside it is very valuable. He hopes it won't take too long to get it free, but he said you should get the wheels off the wagon.'

'I have dug out two wheels,' Zluty said, curious about the singing device, but rather than ask questions, he said, 'I will dig out the other two and you can help me take them off.'

It did not take long to uncover the remaining wheels, but getting all of them off was harder than he had expected, even with Bily's help, because the fastenings were frozen. Bily had to pour hot water on to loosen them, then they had to wait until the metal cooled enough to be touched.

Zluty was eager to see how it would be to drag the wagon over the coldwhites. He thought it would move very easily and lightly. The tiresome thing was that *they* would have to forge a path through the coldwhites, pulling the wagon. But with luck, they would pack down harder by the morrow.

When the porridge was done, Bily bid him fetch the diggers. Zluty set off at a trot along the furrow, thinking they would have to start being more frugal with their use of firenuts. They would need fire to cook and even to melt water to drink, if there was no running water in the cold North, and firenuts did not grow there. Of course, the memory scents carried by the diggers might tell them where to find food and running water, but it would be better if they moved fast enough that their supplies would last the whole of their journey around the mountains.

10

The Makers device was further away than he had thought, and when Zluty got closer he realised he had misjudged the distance because he had not understood how big it was.

Approaching it he slowed, amazed at the size of it, and marvelling how, in all the years he and Bily had lived on the plain surrounded by metal devices, they had never wondered where they came from. The most he had ever done was to pick up the odd piece of metal that might prove useful. Had the devices failed to interest them because the metal in them did not call to him or Bily?

The smooth curved bulk of the machine hid the diggers from sight, as did the coldwhites forming a great drift about its base, but when Zluty circled round, he saw that the diggers had tunnelled into the drift. Ducking his head to enter the tunnel, he found the diggers had hollowed out a little rough cave at the side of the device. There was a lantern set to one side, lighting it, and Zluty was astonished to realise that the device was buried in the earth. This meant it was even bigger than it looked.

He was reminded of the great bowl-shaped dip in the ground in the Northern Forest. For years he had collected mushrooms in darkness, never seeing that the dip was part of an enormous broken metal object half sunk in earth and overgrown with plants, until it was lit with skystones.

Going closer to the device, Zluty saw there was a square opening in it at ground level. He could see the tip of Flugal's tail sticking out. The rest of the digger was hidden inside the device. Zluty heard a movement to one side, and turned to see Semmel rummaging in a bag of tools. Catching sight of him, she called to Flugal that Zluty had come.

The he digger immediately backed out of the opening and beamed at him delightedly. 'Ra!' he cried cheerfully, sitting back on his haunches.

'Do you know what this is for?' Zluty asked, gesturing to the machine.

'Makers making this to taste the earth this side of the sky crack,' the he digger answered.

Totally confused, Zluty said, 'Bily says come and eat before the porridge is spoiled.'

'Almost getting piece free,' Flugal said, sounding rather fed up.

'Can I help?' Zluty asked, expecting to be refused.

To his surprise, Flugal motioned for Zluty to look into the opening. He stepped aside and Zluty got down onto his hands and knees and peered inside the device. It was dark, but another lantern had been hung on a jutting bit of its innards, illuminating them.

Flugal reached past him to point to the piece he had been trying to get free.

It was a small, round metal shape with smoothed, curved edges, save for two bits sticking out of it. There were metal wires hanging loose from the device above and below the metal piece and Zluty supposed they had been attached to it.

'Nothing holds it in place now, but I cannot get it free, *Zchloo-tee*,' Flugal said, explaining that his paws were too small to get a proper grip. He showed Zluty a tool he had been using, which had strong jaws that opened and closed. Unfortunately, the roundness of the object made it hard for the jaws to grip.

Zluty lay on his belly and wriggled right up to the opening in the device. It was too small for him to fit both his head and arm through at the same time. So after looking in to fix in his mind the position of the piece Flugal wanted, he put in his hand and reached out until his fingers found its round shape. He got a good grip and twisted. It shifted unwillingly, then stopped.

Zluty shifted his grip and twisted the piece again, as hard as he could. After a slight resistance, it came loose in his hand quite suddenly. It was a good deal heavier than he expected and he almost dropped it.

To his astonishment, the metal piece seemed *to tremble*. He froze, but it lay heavy and still in his palm. He closed his fingers about it and began to ease back out of the opening.

Sitting up, Zluty studied his prize. The metal object had markings, as did many of the Makers devices and machines, but was otherwise smooth. He noticed one of the bits that stuck out of it was sharp, and looking more closely, he realised the top of it had snapped off.

Flugal touched the broken bit regretfully. 'It broke when I was trying to get it free,' he said. 'It cannot singing now.'

Zluty stared at him, thinking of what Bily had said. 'Is it . . . was it alive?'

'It is alive,' Flugal said, taking it from him and turning it in his paws to examine it. 'No use to taking bits that are not alive.'

Zluty drew in a breath, then he said slowly, 'When you say bits of the Makers machines are *alive*, you mean they work separately from the thing you took them from?'

'Yes,' Flugal said absently.

Semmel had come close, too, and she added gravely, 'Things have their own purposes, *Zchloo-tee*, before the Makers plan gobbles them up. That device could sing, but it was not why the Makers wanted it. They made it serve their plan.'

'But . . .' Zluty began, then stopped, not sure what he wanted to say. Finally he said, 'That . . . that piece of metal shivered in my hand when I got it free.'

Flugal gave him a strange look. 'That is not possible, *Zchloo-tee*. Maybe you bumped it on an unseen something.'

Zluty wanted to believe Flugal, yet the memory of the device trembling like a living creature in his hand was too vivid. The three of them walked together back along the furrow to the wagon, where they sat obediently on the groundsheets

Bily had laid out. The fire was now no more than a few embers and as Bily served them a bowl each, he pointed out reproachfully that the porridge had got lumpy. Eating a mouthful, Zluty insisted that it was perfectly delicious and who said porridge must always be smooth anyway?

Bily looked so startled at this that Zluty forgot his unease about the device and burst out laughing.

By the time they set off again, the sky had lightened to a pale brightness that blended into the shining blanket of coldwhites so that it was impossible to make out the horizon line. Zluty did not fret at the lateness of their departure when he discovered how smoothly and lightly the wagon moved over the coldwhites, and despite his fears, he and Bily were able to run without much difficulty, pulling the wagon after them. Indeed, it moved so quickly that they had to shift both towropes to the sides of the wagon so they could slow it when it threatened to pull them off their feet. The diggers were unable to keep up, so Zluty suggested they ride.

The Monster was awake again but there was no time to question it now. Yet as they had packed up the breakfast things and prepared to go on, Zluty saw that it was sitting alertly, and wondered why. Perhaps it was only that the soothing potion had worn off enough for the Monster to realise it was only a matter of time before it would sicken again, and now it understood there would be no help for it, save in the Velvet City.

As they sped ever North, the cloud cover thinned and the day brightened so much that the coldwhites began to give off a dazzling glare. Zluty felt sure the sun would break through at last. Indeed, for the first time he could *see* it as a very bright patch behind the clouds, but it was not high above the horizon, and before long it began to sink without ever having pierced the clouds. The white sky dimmed to grey, and a cold wind began to blow from the North. All at once the brief day was drawing to an end.

Coldwhites began to fall and suddenly the wind was full of them. They stopped to drop down the awning sides and fasten them, then pushed on, he and Bily leaning into the bullying wind, keeping their heads down to protect their faces. The wind pushing against the awning slowed them and made it hard to direct the wagon forward, but Zluty was determined not to stop until it was true dark. It worried him that they had not reached the Raincage that was supposed to mark the halfway point in their journey, for they had gone though more than half of their supplies.

When he mentioned it to Flugal, who had got back into place with Semmel at the front of the wagon, the he digger admitted that the ancestral memory scents connected to the Raincage were generations old and might have weakened.

It was still not quite full dark when they had to stop, for the wind was fairly howling and the air so thick with flying coldwhites that Zluty's senses were muddled. They could no longer see the guiding bulk of the mountains.

'A blizzard comes,' Semmel said, wide-eyed, when they came inside the wagon.

'A *coldwhite* blizzard,' Flugal reassured Zluty, seeing the look on his face. 'We must anchor the wagon.'

Zluty got out and hastily mounded coldwhites around the wheels, stamping them down hard before he retreated gladly into the wagon. They made do with nuts and dried berries for supper because the wind was so strong that, when it shook the wagon, the cooking table might be toppled. They kept one lantern lit because its tiny flame was enclosed and it could be hung so it would not fall.

All of them were wide awake, even the Monster, but the noise made by the wind, the creaking metal of the wagon and the flap of the awning made it quite impossible to talk. Once again Zluty had to abandon his resolution to question the Monster about the Velvet City. Wearily, he sat on his bedding, watching Bily and Semmel rearrange the interior of the wagon, communicating by gesture alone. In the swinging lantern light it looked as if they were doing some odd dance, and Zluty was reminded of the she digger's dance the previous night, the sweet greenish smoke writhing around her as if it were alive. He wondered what she had done with the ashes, but there was no way to ask until the blizzard ended. He lay down on his bedding and closed his eyes, letting the monotonous keening of the storm lull him to sleep.

A forceful buffet of wind woke him.

Zluty sat up properly and looked around, feeling alarmed and groggy at the same time. The others were asleep and he could hear that the blizzard was still raging outside, coldwhites slapping against the awning. He would have to dig the wagon out of a drift again in the morning before they could go on. His cloak had been spread over him and he was glad of it, for despite the warmth of the Monster, it was very cold and his breath came out in little puffs of mist.

He noticed the Monster was moving restlessly, its paws twitching again. It might be dreaming, or maybe it was beginning to sicken again. For Bily's sake as much as the Monster's he hoped he was wrong, for his soft-hearted brother would feel the Monster's pain as if it were his own.

Zluty closed his eyes, but his mind drifted on the edge of sleep. His thoughts flew North; not to the icy end of the mountain range that was their destination, but back in time to the great Northern Forest. The last time he had gone there he had been trapped by the stone storm and had ventured deeper than ever before with the shining skystones to light his way.

He remembered that walk, and the burnt place at the end of the broken stone wall, where he had discovered the bones of the huge dead creature inside its enormous metal egg. He and Bily had learned that they had come through the sky crack in an egg, which meant they had to have been sent. Yet they were not part of the Makers plan, so who had sent them?

Zluty wondered if they could have been sent through the sky crack by a Maker *before* the Makers had got interested in what lay beyond it; before they had made their plan and started putting metal into things that lived. Of course, that would mean the Makers had put them through the sky crack with all of the other things they had not wanted.

This thought made Zluty open his eyes, but he soon closed them again because he did not know how their egg had come to be on the plain, and he was unlikely ever to know. It was a mystery, just as the little metal egg that he had found was a mystery, and Redwing was a mystery.

Zluty felt suddenly certain that all of the different mysteries were connected, like the digger burrows with their many separate huts and separate entrances that led to a connected central network of tunnels and burrows. The digger huts looked like separate dwellings, but hidden under the earth, they were linked to all of the others. Perhaps if he could solve just one mystery, the answer would lead him to understand all the others.

The wind gave the wagon another very hard jerk but Zluty barely felt it. He was sinking into sleep again, and into a dream of soaring through the flyway.

two

THE COLDWAY

11

Semmel shook Bily hard and he opened his eyes to find her bent over him, mouth moving, paws swooping. She was trying to tell him something, but the wind was still howling outside, making it impossible to hear, and he was too muddle-headed to make his mind quiet enough to understand her thoughts. He sat up, rubbing his eyes and trying to gather his wits. The blanket fell away and the shock of the cold struck him like a slap, bringing him wide awake.

He noticed Zluty pulling on his cloak. He was talking to Flugal, and Bily saw that the door and the awning above it were open, wind blowing cold fluffs inside. That was why it was so cold.

'What is happening?' he called out to Semmel, but she did not hear him, and her attention was fixed on Flugal, who was gesturing urgently to Zluty.

'The wagon came unanchored in the night,' the Monster's dark soft voice spoke into his mind.

Dismayed, Bily turned to look into its yellow eyes. It was sitting upright for the first time in ages, the wind making little trails in its dense short fur and catching the silky tufts on its ear tips, bending them like stalks of sweetgrass.

'We were blown South?' Bily asked.

'North,' the Monster answered. 'Very far North. The wind changed in the night. Probably that is what dislodged us.'

Zluty came to Bily, his expression anguished. 'I did not push enough snow in front of the wagon because the wind was blowing from the North. I didn't think of it turning and coming from the South!'

'It does not matter,' Semmel said, patting his arm. 'The wagon only got its nose stuck in a pile of coldwhites.'

'It was not damaged?' Bily asked Zluty incredulously.

'The diggers don't think so, and I am sure they are right. If it had crashed into anything we would have been woken, but I want to go and see if there is any damage.'

'I will come too,' Bily said, but Zluty shook his head.

'The diggers are coming with me. You had better stay with the Monster,' Zluty said. He glanced over at it and added quietly, 'It was very restless in the night.'

Bily heaved a sigh and wrung his hands. 'The soothing potion is wearing off. I have the recipe and all the ingredients I need to make more, only I can't make it while we are travelling.'

'Don't worry,' Zluty said. 'We have been lucky. The wind might easily have driven us headlong into the mountain. The wagon could have been destroyed or we might have been hurt. Instead, we have been blown closer to the end of the mountains.'

Bily nodded doubtfully. 'What about the Raincage?'

Zluty shrugged. 'We have probably passed it.

Semmel thinks she will be able to work out how far we have come when she can see the mountains and touch them. That is why she is coming with Flugal and me.'

'Shut the awning to keep the warm in. We will come back soonly,' Flugal signalled as they left, slamming the door behind them. Bily got up to fasten the awning after them, though there was not much warmth left to keep in.

He tried to look outside as he fastened the awning, but cold fluffs were blowing too thick and fast to see anything. It was not day, but he fancied that it was very close to dawn. He noticed a little fur of cold fluffs had formed along the bits of the metal frame that had been exposed to the blizzard wind, and along the tiny strands of the spider's web, as if the world was growing a pelt of ice.

By the time he got the awning shut, he was shuddering with cold. He wished he could light a fire, but it would be too dangerous with the wind rocking the wagon. Besides, their supply of firenuts and food was diminishing badly.

He put on his cloak and went back to the Monster. It was still sitting upright, its yellow eyes narrowed as if listening to something.

It seemed not to notice him and he was suddenly shy of interrupting its thoughts. He climbed back into his bedding and tried to think how to ask if it was feeling poorly. He could not tell if it was hotter than usual because the air was so cold, but he was glad of the warmth of its body, and snuggled closer. Semmel had said that it would grow colder each day they travelled North, yet it was impossible to believe it could get any colder than it was. Oh, how he longed for hot sunshine and bright colour.

Bily's eyes began to droop and, in spite of everything, he fell into a doze. He dreamed of a voice, bidding him urgently to find the lock that his key would fit. The urgency of the voice was so strong that he felt alarmed.

'I don't know what you mean? What lock? What door?' he cried.

'Bily,' said the Monster, in his mind.

I am dreaming, Bily thought, drowsily.

'Yes, but wake now,' said the Monster, with the hint of a growl.

Bily opened his eyes and found the Monster looking down at him. 'There is something outside,' it said.

Bily felt his bones turn to ice. 'Is it Monks?' he

whispered. Then, with a dry mouth, 'Is it Makers?'

'The Makers cannot come through the sky crack until it is widened enough,' the Monster said, but its voice was distracted. It was staring up at the awning, its eyes burning.

Bily thought with a great lurch of fright of the dark shadow he had seen moving across the face of the mountain. Then he remembered Zluty and the diggers were outside. Almost crying with dismay, he scrambled to his feet. Going to the side of the wagon, he unlaced the awning and looked out. Cold fluffs were still blowing, but less thickly. He could see that it was day, though he could not tell how late it was, nor could he see any sign of the others.

'I can't have slept long for the others were just going out to look at the wagon,' he muttered. Then a truly dreadful thought occurred to him. He turned to the Monster. 'What if Zluty and the diggers have been found by whatever you can smell outside?'

The Monster said nothing, but its ears were twitching so that the long silken tufts wavered this way and that. They both froze at the sound of a long, low rumbling noise, like the noise of thunder, rolling across the plain.

'Is it rocks falling down the mountain?' Bily whispered, remembering the one that had fallen when Zluty had been getting water.

'It is not rocks falling. It is a hunting cry,' the Monster said in its velvety voice.

'Something is hunting us?' Bily whispered fearfully.

'It is hunting *me*,' the Monster said, very softly.

'How much further?' Zluty yelled back to Flugal, beginning to worry about Bily. Flugal had told him they would be back soon, but they had been walking for at least twenty minutes.

Flugal and Semmel had started out walking ahead of him, guided by the pouch of memory scents that had alerted them to the nearness of the Raincage. But the snow had got so deep that they had trouble and Zluty had taken the lead. Now they seemed not to hear him, marching along behind him, arms linked for support as they pushed into the wind and coldwhites.

He was about to shout his question again, when Flugal signalled that they were close. Zluty sighed in frustration and turned South again, pushing through the coldwhites and bending his head to keep the icy wind from burning his cheeks.

They were backtracking because the scent memories had told Semmel this was the way to the Raincage. They had been inspecting the wagon hull for damage when Semmel came running up.

She had left them to go and put her paw on the mountain so as to learn how far North they had come. She had been so agitated that Zluty had been unable to understand her, and it was Flugal who explained.

'The Raincage is very nearful, Semmel says. We must go, for bringing the scent memories to it will release more needful knowings.'

Zluty had gone to let Bily know, but found him sleeping, so he told the Monster about the Raincage. The Monster had been sitting up, alert, but had made no response. Now, Zluty worried it had not heard him and that Bily would wake and be frightened that they had not returned.

Zluty tried to take bigger strides, knowing it would be silly to turn back and waste precious daylight. After all, the Monster was with Bily, even if it did not remember Zluty saying they were going to see the Raincage. And unlocking the scent memories was vital to their survival. Besides all else, he had to admit he was very curious about what a Raincage could be.

Slowing to dig through a thick drift of cold-whites, he thought of the wagon and hoped the hull was not damaged underneath. He and Flugal had examined it, but they would not be able to see clearly until they had got it free of the drift of coldwhites. It was lucky that was where the wind had blown it, and he shuddered to think of all the dreadful things that might have come of their accidental journey through the night. If they had crashed, it would have been his fault because he didn't put enough coldwhites around the wheels.

'Nothing bad happened,' Zluty told himself sternly. 'Stop making a fuss and be more careful.'

Surprised the diggers had not caught up, he glanced back and saw they had stopped. They were not looking at him. Their heads were tilted, their ears twitching. They were listening to something, he realised, and as he straightened, he became aware of another noise under the sound of the wind moaning across the plain. It was the sound of water falling.

Semmel looked at him, black eyes shining. 'The Raincage is very near, *Zchloo-tee*.' She pointed to the mountain.

He turned to look in puzzlement at the mountain rising almost straight up beside them, its dark flank too sheer and steep for any coldwhites to cling to. But when he looked back at the diggers to ask what they meant, he saw they were running directly at the mountain. Seeing them vanish into it, he set off after them with a cry of alarm, only to find there was a narrow crevice that had been all but invisible.

He had to turn sideways to get into it, but to his relief it widened almost immediately into a tunnel. He made haste to catch up to the diggers, who were moving fast now there were no coldwhites underfoot. Semmel was leading the way and Flugal lifted his paw to signal to Zluty that the scent memories had told Semmel the passage would bring them to the cave, where they would find the Raincage.

The deeper they went into the mountain, the more muffled the sound of rushing water was. Zluty glanced back and could just see a strip of grey sky through the dark, narrow opening. When he turned back, the diggers had vanished around a bend. He sped up until he could see them, standing transfixed at the end of the passage.

Moving towards them, Zluty was startled to find that the walls reflected the dull radiance of the skystones on his staff. He touched the nearest wall and found it was slicked with a hard coat of ice.

He reached the diggers and crouched down to see past them. The opening at the end of the tunnel looked into a narrow cavern. Daylight was flowing down into it from somewhere high up. The light reflected off the dark walls and he realised they too were encased in a skin of ice, which explained why it was so cold.

The diggers climbed down into the cavern, which widened as it ran round out of sight to the right. Zluty crawled out and stood up to follow the diggers, who were leaping lightly down the sloping, uneven floor. He picked his way carefully after them, using his staff to steady himself, for the ground was icy, too. He had not gone far when he realised that the cavern was actually an immense tunnel and that he could hear the sound of rushing water again, muffled and far away.

The air grew wetter and wetter. Soon his exposed fur was beaded with water droplets and his teeth were chattering. He would not have been surprised to see the drops turn to ice.

'How much further?' he asked, or tried to ask, for his numb lips would not obey him. His head felt thick and he wondered if the cold was making him a bit stupid. He was about to ask again, when he realised the diggers had stopped at another bend, and were looking at something out of his vision.

Panting, he reached Semmel's side in time to hear her say reverently, 'It is the Raincage.'

12

Dim grey daylight poured down the centre of the cavern from an opening high above, into a milky-green pool of water. The water threw the light onto the iced walls and lit the fine mist floating in the air. There were immense shards of green ice sticking up out of the water and lying around the edges of the pool. The ground was covered in a fine cold black sand.

An enormous glistening fall of water hung frozen above the pool. Drops slipped down the many long sharp icicles and into the pool, sounding like rain. Each drop must add a slick of glistening ice to the long daggers of frozen water, lengthening and sharpening them before falling away, thought Zluty in wonderment. That was how the icefall had formed.

'It is a great loveliness,' Flugal murmured, and Semmel gave a little chitter of agreement.

Zluty could still hear the distant roar of water, and he asked the diggers if they knew what it was.

Semmel looked at the icefall and then said in a dreamy voice, 'A great spring breaks the head of the mountain to get free, and flows fast and strong and wild until it spills from the mountains and runs across the land to the Edgeless Sea.' She pointed to the Raincage, and said in her normal voice, 'This comes from that stream. Some of its water falls through holes in the mountain. The way down is longful and the water turns mistful. The mist makes the air and walls wet and sends drips down to the meltwater pool that freeze. That is the telling of the Raincage, *Zchloo-tee*.'

'Do the memory scents say how your people found this place?' Zluty asked her.

'Running and hiding,' Flugal said. 'Must be.'

'*Bee-lee* will want to see,' Semmel said, and Zluty

realised with surprise that, like him, it pleased her
to please Bily. She was right, of course, for no telling could conjure the wonder of the Raincage. And
yet it would devour much of the remaining day to

go back to the wagon and fetch him back. Maybe Semmel could bring Bily here while he and Flugal dug out the wagon and made it ready to go on.

'We should go back,' he said loudly, suddenly worried about Bily. They had been whispering until now, for no particular reason. But Flugal quickly shushed him, looking alarmed.

'Scent memories saying that sometimes noise causes bits of Raincage to shatter,' Flugal whispered. 'Very dangerful.' He pointed to the jagged bits of ice in the pool and around it.

Zluty swallowed, imagining the icefall shattering and sending sharp spikes in all directions. All three of them turned to look again at the glittering fall of frozen water suspended above the meltwater pool. Zluty thought that it was the most dangerously beautiful thing he had ever seen.

Coming out of the long crevice into the daylight and the icy wind, Zluty realised that the cold-whites had ceased falling and the wind, though still blowing strongly, was now coming from the South-east. That would help them when they set off.

They hurried along the furrow they had made earlier, the diggers taking the lead.

'It is a good thing the wind is behind us, for we must move as fast as we can now,' Zluty said. 'If the Raincage is only halfway, we have a long way to go to the end of the mountains.'

Semmel looked back at him and smiled. 'It will not take us longly to make that journey, *Zchloo-tee*.'

Before he could think what to say to this, Flugal was pointing ahead, saying he could see the wagon. Zluty looked North and was very relieved to see that the wagon *was* visible.

'The Raincage was a wondrous thing, but if I looked too long it would steal the knowing out of me,' Flugal said.

Semmel gave him a quick, sharp look. 'The memory scents warn of its power to do that. They tell that the diggers used its power to lock the memory scents from the North so there could be no knowing of them until they were brought North again. They will not tell why until we come to the place where the memory scents were made.'

'But we need them to tell us about finding food in the North,' Zluty said, alarmed.

Flugal gave him a slightly reproachful look and Semmel said, 'There are many layers to the memory scents, *Zchloo-tee*. Those that are needful will come as we go further Northly.'

Zluty suppressed a worried sigh. They definitely did not have enough food to last them to the end of the mountain range. And if they could not round the mountains before the season of ice blizzards came, they would die of cold, if not of hunger, without the help of the memory scents. If they were sensible, they would turn back to the digger settlement at once. But Bily would never agree to that, for the digger potion-maker had made it clear that the Monster must be returned to the Velvet City by the first days of Spring, or die.

'Do not be fearful, *Zchloo-tee*. Soonly, we can use special device gifted to you to make journey go very swifty,' Flugal said, a flicker of excitement in his bright eyes.

Zluty was thrilled that he would soon discover the purpose of the device lashed to the side of the wagon. But *why* had they not already made use of it if it could make them go faster? He knew better than to ask. Probably the diggers had feared missing the Raincage.

Zluty felt a rush of relief as they drew closer to the wagon, its nose pushed into the drift of cold-whites at the foot of the great frowning bulk of the mountain.

'Something is wrongful,' Flugal said, stopping.

Zluty looked at the digger, startled by his tone. Flugal's eyes were fixed on the wagon. Zluty squinted. Then he saw it. There was something odd about the shape of the awning at one end. It looked as if it had collapsed. He had a sudden sick thought that a boulder had come plummeting down from the mountain and landed on the wagon.

'The wind probably just changed and tore the

awning off its frame,' he muttered, pushing the horrid thought away. But if that was so, where was Bily? Dry-mouthed with fear, Zluty threw down his staff and ran past the diggers, calling out to Bily. He heard Flugal call his name, but he did not look back. By the time he got close enough to the wagon to call out, Zluty was stumbling and gasping.

'Bily!' he cried out in a rasping croak.

There was no response. He saw that part of the awning had been torn right away and the back of the wagon was completely exposed. The door was half buried in a new drift of coldwhites, and he had to force his way in.

'Bily!' he whispered, seeing his brother was not inside the wagon.

Then Zluty gave a huff of relief. Bily had probably just gone looking for *them* when the coldwhites began falling hard, and then the awning had blown off. He would never leave the injured Monster alone and exposed to the weather.

At that thought a hole seemed to open up in Zluty's stomach. He turned to look at the place where the Monster slept.

The Monster was gone, too.

13

It was impossible, Zluty told himself sternly. The Monster could barely stand and would scarcely have been able to drag itself from the wagon. There would be no reason for it to do so, unless Bily had been in trouble and had cried out.

Heart thumping, Zluty climbed up onto the side of the wagon where the awning had been torn away, and looked North. There was no sign of the Monster or Bily. Worse, the snow was pristine – there was not a single footprint or paw print.

Utterly bewildered, Zluty looked East, but there was nothing at all but coldwhites and grey sky for

as far as he could see. He walked around the rim
of the wagon to look South and saw only Semmel
and Flugal still making their way along the furrow
towards him.

Zluty turned to the black flank of the nearest
mountain looming over the wagon. He leaned back
until he could just make out its white cap of coldwhites, but there was no sign of movement.

'Bily!' he cried, and saw several powdery showers of coldwhites fall, but there was no response.

He turned and leapt down into the wagon, and began frantically searching for a clue as to what had happened to his brother and the ailing Monster. The bedding, normally smoothed out, was all humped up as if it had been picked up and then dropped. He studied the torn awning, and now saw that it had been ripped cleanly from top to bottom.

'As if a knife was used,' Zluty muttered as Flugal said his name softly. He turned to look at the he digger with a sudden wild hope that Flugal would know what had happened. But the little digger was gazing around with bewildered dismay.

He said, '*Zchloo-tee*, there is being a smell of strangeness.'

'A smell?' Zluty echoed, heart pounding. He sniffed but the cold had all but made his nose useless.

Flugal went to sniff at the Monster's bedding and then he climbed up to sniff the awning. 'It is the smell of a beast.'

Zluty went to the side of the wagon and looked up into the digger's earnest little face. 'A beast, Flugal? A Monk?'

Flugal shook his head. 'Something I have not smelled before,' he said, and this time Zluty took in the meaning of the words.

'What sort of beast could carry Bily and the Monster off without leaving any tracks?' he asked. Then he thought of the huge bones in the metal egg in the Northern Forest, and of the Monster saying beasts went there in Winter.

'*Zchloo-tee*! Flugal!' Semmel called from outside.

The cry had come from the North and they both went to the edge of the wagon and looked out. Semmel was some distance away, beckoning for them to come to her. It was not until they were pushing through the coldwhites to join her that Zluty saw she was standing on the edge of a wide dip that had not been visible because of the radiant whiteness.

And it was not until he reached her that he saw the dip was an enormous paw print.

For the first time in his life, Zluty fainted out of sheer horror.

Bily's hands were beginning to slip. He gritted his teeth and tried to grip the tufts of fur in his fingers more tightly, willing the Monster to wake. Its

limbs hung so limp that he was afraid of what the
Nightbeast had done when it closed its jaws on the
Monster's neck.

The first they had seen of the dreadful beast were
its terrible claws cutting through the awning as if it

was made of paper. Then it pushed its black head in through the gap. It had been so big and dark that it seemed to Bily as if the night itself looked in. Its fierce green eyes had fastened on the Monster lying helpless on its bedding. Then the Nightbeast had opened its mouth to reveal a red throat and tongue, and teeth like white daggers, as it stretched out its head towards the Monster.

Bily had thrown himself forward, determined to fend off those terrible teeth, but the Monster's tail lashed out, swatting him out of danger. Lying half stunned, Bily had thought the beast would bite off the Monster's head with one fearsome snap, but instead it had closed its teeth in the flesh at the back of the Monster's neck and lifted it as if it weighed no more than a digger youngling. The Monster had not yowled or fought or resisted in any way, but had hung limp as the Nightbeast withdrew.

There had been no thought at all in Bily's mind when he scrambled to his feet and threw himself across the wagon to catch hold of the Monster's dangling back paw, grasping hold of its silky fur. Half blinded by a swirl of cold fluffs, he had a fleeting glimpse of the Nightbeast looming overhead, black and impossibly huge. Then it bunched its muscles and sprang away from the wagon, twisting lithely so that it landed close to the foot of the mountain. The jolt of landing almost dislodged Bily, but he clung grimly. Then the Nightbeast sprang at the sheer black mountainside.

Bily remembered the mindless terror he had felt, but the Nightbeast landed with all fours, its sharp claws finding a hold in the sheer slope. Somehow, impossibly, it bunched its muscles and leapt up again and then again. Bily had feared it meant to run straight up the side of the mountain, but with one more spring it reached a narrow ledge that ran just below the place where the mountains split into sharp white-capped peaks.

The Nightbeast had been moving Northward along the ledge ever since, in a swift, gliding, low-bellied crawl, occasionally leaping where the ledge had broken away, or where a mound of cold fluffs blocked the way. Bily knew when it would leap because it would pause to gather itself before bunching its powerful muscles to spring. Each time it paused, he held on as tight as he could to the Monster's leg.

But at each leap his grip slipped a little more.

He feared it would only take one more leap, and he would plummet straight down the mountain to his death. He dared not imagine how high they had come. He had looked out only once, not long after the Nightbeast reached the ledge, and he had seen the white plain far below him running as far as he could see in all directions. Then the ledge had begun to angle upward slightly, so that they had been climbing, until they came to a place where mist rolled down from the mountain-top. Now, Bily could see nothing but cloud.

He had no idea where the Nightbeast was taking the Monster, but his only hope of rescuing it depended upon the enormous creature stopping to rest, or to eat or drink. He had thought at first that the Monster must be its intended supper, but why not eat it at once? To carry it so far across this terrain was a feat even for a beast of such incredible size and strength.

That had led Bily to wonder if the beast had taken the Monster to feed its younglings. This was a horrid thought and he hoped its brood were very far away.

If only it would stop for a drink. Bily had managed to lick up some cold fluffs from his fur, but he was still dreadfully thirsty. And the Nightbeast could not even do that with the Monster in its mouth. Bily had decided that it must have a stopping place in mind. The danger would come when it did stop.

He was sure it had not noticed him, and he must take care to remain hidden, but he was worried about the Monster, for it had not moved the whole time they had been travelling. If only he could find a cave just big enough for him and the Monster to hide. But how to get the Monster into a cave if it could not help him? And even if he succeeded, and the Nightbeast went away, how could he get the Monster back down the mountain along the narrow ledge and down that impossible sheer drop where the Nightbeast had leapt straight up.

Nor could he hope that Zluty and the diggers would come to save them. He knew how frightened his brother would have been to find them vanished. Zluty would want to track the Nightbeast, but once he saw where its tracks led, he would realise it was impossible. He would have no choice but to turn back and use the Monk's ascending machine to get into the mountains, or go around the end of the mountains and come up from the other side of the range. He thought Zluty would choose to go on, and he prayed that once they got out of the clouds he would see the wagon continuing North, even if it was only a bright red speck in the distance.

14

Zluty was sitting on a rock, thinking about Bily.

They had searched for more tracks in widening circles about the wagon, looking for clues to what had happened to Bily. It was not until the diggers climbed up the stony flank of the nearest mountain that they found more tracks, and understood that was where the beast had gone. Zluty had not been able to climb far because the slope was too steep, but the diggers were smaller and there were many tiny juts and ledges they could cling to. It was they who had found claw marks in the stone that matched the giant paw print they had found in the coldwhites. They had followed the scratches high enough to see a ledge that they believed the enormous beast had been making for. They had been unable to get to the ledge because the mountain became too sheer even for them, but it ran North.

It seemed clear the beast had taken the Monster, but Zluty had not been sure of what had happened to Bily until he found another giant paw print in the coldwhites on the rim of the wagon, and beside it, the trace of a small footprint.

It had not been difficult to guess what had transpired, then. The great beast had leapt onto the wagon and had clawed through the awning to reach in and lift the Monster out. Bily had jumped after it and caught hold of the Monster's tail or paw. It was exactly the sort of thing Bily would do, driven by love and loyalty.

Which meant Bily was with the Monster and the great beast. If it was taking the Monster back to its lair to eat it, Bily would try to defend it. And Bily would be eaten.

Zluty buried his head in his hands and wept.

Semmel came to him. She took his face in her

little paws to make him look at her. Staring into her kindly eyes, the storm of grief in his mind quietened enough for him to hear her when she spoke.

'Whatever happened to *Bee-lee* and the Listener, *Zchloo-tee* dearling, they will not come back here, and each moment we stay stopped, they will go further away. We must go after them.'

'How?' Zluty cried, gesturing to the mountain.

'The beast that took them will not go up and up,' Semmel said. 'The ice blizzards are too dangerful. It will stay on the mountain's side to be safely.'

'If it takes them to its lair . . .'

Semmel twitched her ears. 'We think it takes Monster to the Velvet City.'

Zluty stared at her. 'To the Velvet City? But why?'

'A beast so bigly cannot have come here without being sent through sky crack,' Flugal said, coming to stand with his mate. 'That means it is part of the Makers plan. Monster is a Listener, so maybe Listeners wanting him back. And asking Makers for helping.'

'You think the Makers sent it to help the Listeners,' Zluty said slowly.

'Maybe sending for that reason,' Semmel said, cautiously.

'What other reason?' Zluty asked.

The diggers exchanged a look, then Semmel said, 'The smell of the beast is in the memory scents. The knowing of that came when I smelled it in the wagon.'

'But . . . what does that mean?' Zluty asked,

then he realised. 'If the smell of the beast is in the memory scents of your ancestors, then it could not just have been sent here by the Makers to find the Monster!'

'Our ancestors made the memory scents in the North. We do not know the why of that, because they did not keep their memories in their heads, but the knowing of the beast is in them,' Semmel said. 'That means it was in the North long ago. Maybe it was sent by the Makers to find our ancestors.'

'But if it has been looking for your ancestors all this time, why did it take the Monster?' Zluty protested.

'Maybe it was lured by our smell in the wagon,' Flugal said.

'In the North we will learn the why of the beast and that will tell us where it took *Bee-lee*,' Semmel said.

Zluty stood up decisively. 'Then let us go North. I have stupidly spent a whole day sitting and thinking. We must go while there is still some daylight.'

'Never stupidness to think before acting,' said Semmel firmly as they made their way together back to the wagon.

The air had got so icy that Bily's ear tips ached and he could not even feel the end of his tail. If only he could pull the hood of the cloak up over his head, but his grip was so precarious that he dared not let go of either hand. The next time the Nightbeast bunched its muscles to jump, he resolved to lock his legs tight around the Monster's paw and reach up to get a better handful of its fur.

If he had been sensible, he would have let go of the Monster at the end of its first leap. He would have done no more than tumble into thick snow. But hours later, as the Nightbeast carried them ever higher up into the mountains, he knew he could not have done it any differently. Because to let go would have been to desert the Monster.

He suddenly remembered how it seemed to sense something before the Nightbeast appeared. And how it had known its deep rumbling roar was a hunting call.

'It hunts *me*,' the Monster had said in its soft dark voice.

But how had it known that? Bily remembered the Monster telling Zluty that its people had stories about immense and dangerous beasts that sought refuge in the Northern Forest in Winter. It had said it did not know the Northern Forest truly existed until it learned that Zluty had been there. Perhaps the Monster had not believed the beasts were real either, until it heard the hunting cry.

If only Bily knew the stories they told about the Nightbeast, he might have a better idea of what to expect. At first he had thought it meant to carry them up to the top of the mountain, but then he remembered the ice blizzards that would be scouring the heights. 'It would not want to face those,' he thought, and then realised with fright that he had spoken his thought aloud.

He waited, heart thumping, but the Nightbeast's gliding progress did not falter. Then a gust of wind blew, and Bily forgot everything else. For the wind parted the thick ruff of fur about the neck of the Nightbeast and he saw the glint of Makers metal.

That meant the Nightbeast must serve the Makers plan. Most likely it had been sent by the Monster's people to bring it back to the Velvet City.

Except the Monster had told him that it was not very important. So why would its people send the Nightbeast to bring it back?

Unless it was the Makers who had sent it.

Bily fought back the storm of fear that assailed him at the thought of being taken to the Makers. After all, he had heard of many kinds of creatures being sent through the sky crack, but never anything about creatures being sent back through it to the Makers world. If the Makers had sent the Nightbeast after the Monster, it was most likely they would have ordered it to be returned to the Velvet City, where its own people might be instructed to punish it.

Bily trembled at the thought, but he told himself sternly that he must be brave, for the sake of the Monster. If the Nightbeast was taking them to the Velvet City, it would have to go around the end of the mountains because of the ice blizzards. That would explain why it was running North. He could not hope they would come down at the end of the mountains and run into Zluty and the diggers, but it was not a bad thing to be taken to the Velvet City. Hadn't they been trying to get the Monster there, after all? And maybe the Listeners would not punish the Monster when they learned it had been ill and injured.

Another possibility occurred to Bily.

The Monster had said that some of its people were Seers who could see the future even as the bees did. What if they had foreseen that the Monster had been injured and so had sent the Nightbeast to rescue it! Perhaps he could reveal himself to it and explain that he and Zluty had been trying to bring the Monster to the Velvet City.

Bily wavered, uncertain, thinking of the Nightbeast's glowing eyes and sharp teeth. Better to stay hidden, he decided. If he could slip away just before the Monster was taken into the Velvet City, he could head North to meet up with Zluty and the diggers, and together they could make a plan to free the Monster.

He strove again to reach the Monster's mind, but it was as limp and lifeless as its limbs. In desperation, very carefully, he tried to reach the mind of the Nightbeast, but there was no open place.

For all he knew its mind had been emptied out and filled up with obedience so that there was no room for listening or thinking, like the poor captured diggers Zluty had described in Stonehouse. He could just imagine the Makers would want to be very sure the Nightbeast could not resist their will, after what had happened with the Cloud Monster.

A chilling thought came to him.

Maybe the Makers did not care that the Monster had been unable to return because of injury. Maybe they cared only that it had defied their bidding, and wished to empty the Monster's mind?

Cold fluffs began to fall. Bily could not see them, but he could feel them slapping coldly and lightly against his skin. He looked up and then down, but the only thing he could see was the narrow ledge and a white mist billowing thickly all around.

He shifted slightly and felt something bump his leg softly. For a moment he was frightened, then he remembered that he had slipped his forage bag over his head when Zluty and the diggers left! It was one bright thing in a dark day, for in it was a little pouch of herbs he could use to sooth the Monster's metal. He thought there might even be a little bag of nuts and seeds in it that they could eat. If only the Nightbeast would stop, he could look. But it glided on and on.

Misty day gave way to dark night and cold fluffs fell so lightly and constantly that Bily felt his fur growing heavy with them, especially his tail.

Bily fought a growing weariness. He knew he must not sleep, but the gliding movement of the Nightbeast and the soft patting of cold fluffs against his cheeks made his eyelids feel so heavy. Each time he blinked it was harder to open his eyes again.

If only there was something to look at, but it was so dark now that there was no more to see than when his eyes were closed.

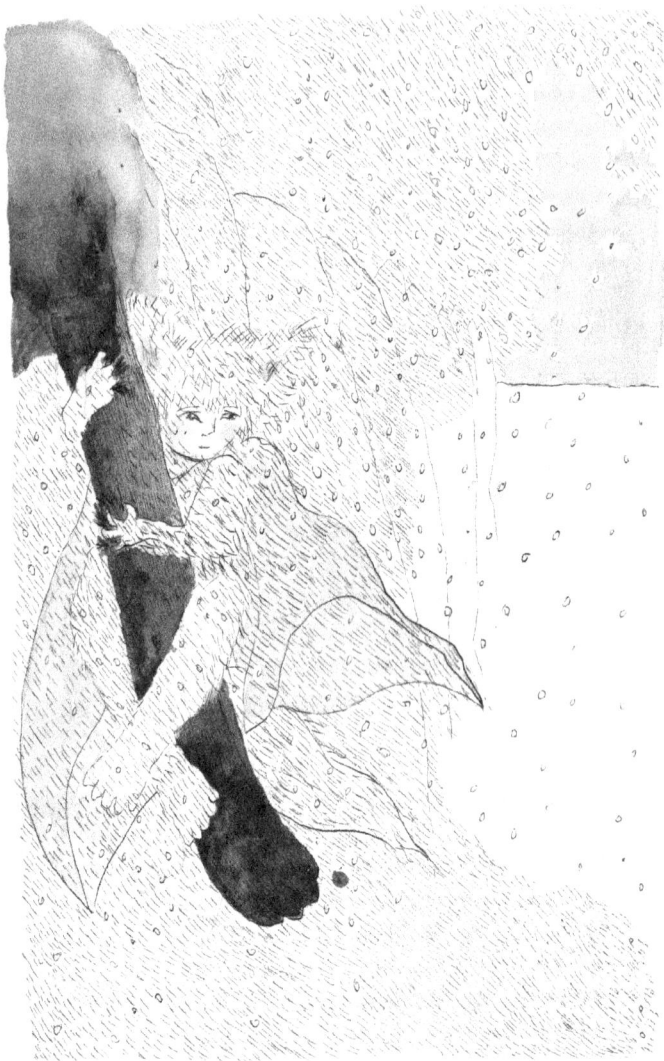

Bily blinked again. A long, slow blink.

He thought how nice to would be to just let his eyes stay closed. He would open his fingers and fall like the cold fluffs fell, softly and quietly all the way down to the bottom of the mountain.

Only he would not land like a cold fluff.

'I would be broken into pieces and Zluty would be alone . . .' he said.

The thought was so lonely and horrible that it roused him from his deadly drowse. He shook his head hard, and blinked over and over.

Then the Nightbeast paused and Bily was instantly alert. He reached up one hand to take a thick tuft of fur, just as the Nightbeast leapt. After a long floating moment, there was the jolt of landing, and Bily shot his other hand out and got a good grip further up the Monster's leg.

Before he could haul himself higher, the Nightbeast leapt again immediately, unexpectedly, and this time down instead of up.

Bily was not prepared, for he had loosened his legs in order to haul himself higher. For one moment, his hands held the full weight of his body, then they lost their grip altogether.

He fell.

15

Zluty was running North over the flat white plain, pulling the wagon after him. It was so light without the weight of the Monster that he had no trouble managing it alone, but he had to be careful because it was properly dark now. The coldwhites had ceased to fall, and there was no mist but also no moon. Luckily the blanket of coldwhites covering the ground gave off a ghostly radiance that let them see well enough to go on, and the wind had scoured the plain so that it was smooth and every dark rock and metal object lying on the whiteness was visible a long way off.

The only risk was the occasional large crack, which was harder to see.

They had decided only one of the diggers would run alongside the wagon, ready to haul on the side towrope if there was a sudden need to stop or to go sharply at an angle to avoid something. The diggers were taking turns since they had to take many more steps than Zluty to cover the same distance, and tired quicker.

At the moment the runner was Semmel. Zluty had to be careful to remember to go slow enough that she could keep up, because whenever he thought about Bily he sped up. He would have preferred both diggers to ride so that he could go faster, but they could not afford to run into anything. The collision with the coldwhite drift had been hard enough to bend the hull a little out of shape so that it did not steer quite true, and he had found a thin crack, as well.

It came to Zluty that if they had not crashed, whatever had taken Bily and the Monster might not have caught them. Then he remembered his feeling of being watched, and the dislodged rock that had fallen, and wondered if the beast had been following them for some time, waiting for its chance.

Zluty glanced up at the mist wreathing the mountains, and willed Bily to be safe. He could only hope the diggers were right, and the beast had been sent to bring the Monster back to the Velvet City. If so, it might easily overlook Bily, who was very small and very good at being quiet. If Bily could only stay with the Monster until they reached the other side of the mountain range, he would be able to escape and come North.

This cheering thought prompted Zluty to suggest using the mysterious device to help them go faster, but the diggers said they had not yet reached the place where it could be used.

When they finally stopped to have a mouthful of water from the urn, and for Flugal to change places with Semmel, Zluty asked Semmel, 'How does the device work? I know we cannot use it yet, but at least I can think about that instead of all the horrible things that might be happening to Bily.'

The diggers exchanged looks of puzzlement.

'We do not have that knowing,' Semmel said.

Zluty stared at her. 'I thought you knew what the device was for,' he stammered.

'We know it is for going fastly, *Zchloo-tee*,' said Semmel earnestly. 'But we do not know how it will work. It was made from plans left by the diggers who returned from the North. The knowing of how to use it will come when we reach the place it can be used, and the memory scents are saying it is nearful.'

'Do they say anything about this place where we can finally use the device?' Zluty said, feeling more and more dismayed.

Semmel nodded. 'It is called the Coldway.'

Zluty was unable to feel much faith in the mysterious device now that he realised the diggers had never used it before and had no idea what it was for, but he would not let himself fall into despair again.

'We would have been there already, but the days grow ever shorter as we go North. Soon there will be no day,' Flugal said, bending to take up the towrope.

Zluty looked at the he digger. 'What do you mean "No day"?'

It was Semmel who answered, taking her place on the prow. 'In the North, each day grows less until the Longful Night comes, and then will come the season of ice blizzards. It will be best to get around the endmost mountains before then, for when the ice blizzards begin, they will not stop until the Longful Night ends.'

'How long is the Longful Night?' Zluty asked.

'I do not have that knowing, *Zchloo-tee*, but there is an old telling that says it depends on the coming of the world's dream,' the she digger said, settling her cloak around her.

Zluty wondered if Semmel meant the small moon that sometimes trailed after the proper moon. Bily might have told her their name for it and she got it muddled. But he could not think what the small moon had to do with a long night.

Thinking of Bily made him dwell again on the danger his brother might be in, and Zluty was glad to go on. He was so busy concentrating on his feet and keeping watch for cracks that it was some time before he noticed the glimmer of stars in the East. The wind must have torn a gap in the clouds!

The world blazed suddenly white and dazzling about him. Zluty saw his shadow stretch out beside him as if it were fleeing to the mountains. The moon was visible for the first time since they had left the digger camp.

Something to the North caught his eye and he turned to see a great silver sword of light lying across the land.

Zluty was so startled that he stopped running. Flugal gave a cry of alarm and threw himself sideways with the towrope, trying desperately to turn the wagon so that it would not run Zluty over.

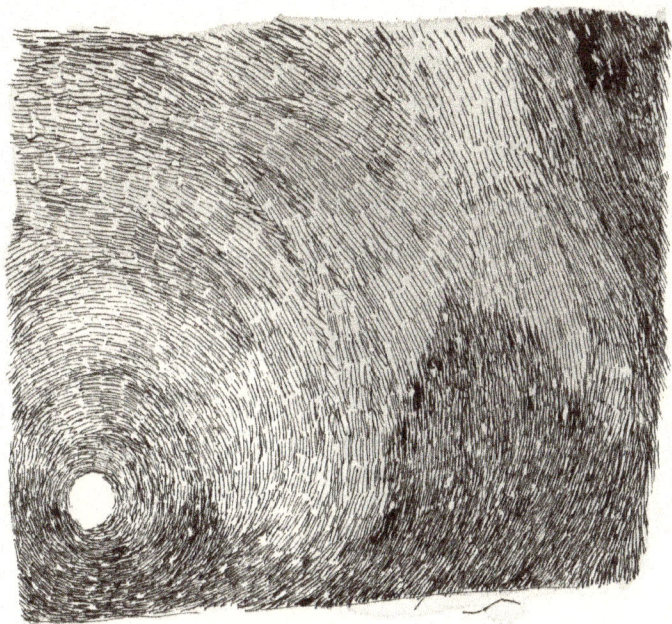

Horrified, Zluty ran to the other side of the wagon to find a shaken Flugal sitting on his tail, looking dazed.

'I'm so sorry,' Zluty told him, helping him to stand. 'I . . . I thought I saw something shining ahead . . .'

'I saw it, too,' Flugal said, dusting the coldwhites fastidiously from his tail. 'It was the moon shining on something,' he added, but the moon had been swallowed by the clouds, and the way ahead was dark again.

'It is the Coldway,' Semmel murmured in a dreamy voice, gazing North from her perch on the prow. 'When we reach it, we can use the device.'

16

'What is the Coldway?' Zluty said, when they set off again.

'We do not know *what* it is,' Semmel said. 'Only that it *is*.'

'But you said . . .' Zluty began.

'Look and see,' Flugal interrupted, pointing North.

Zluty squinted and finally saw what the diggers had seen with their sharp eyes: a grey road that ran straight East out of the mountains, and across their path, before curving North.

'That is the Coldway,' Flugal said.

'Who would build a road *here*?' Zluty muttered, wondering how a road could have reflected the moonlight so brightly.

'No one built it,' Semmel murmured in the soft, almost sleepy voice she used whenever the memory scents stirred. They seemed to affect her more than Flugal, though the diggers took turns wearing the pouch containing them around their necks.

It was not until they reached the side of the road that Zluty discovered it was made of ice!

Flugal unhooked the lantern from the front of the wagon and climbed down the bank of cold-whites onto the ice road. 'There is water under the iciness,' he called.

Zluty understood then. The Coldway was not a road, but a river that had frozen!

He fetched the net socks Flugal had made, pulled them on and then fastened the tow-rope around his waist, before climbing down beside Flugal. He stepped carefully onto the ice, for he was a good deal heavier than the digger. As soon as he was standing on it, he could tell that it was very thick, though he could

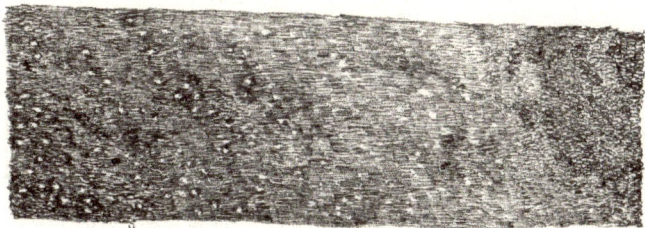

hear the eerie muffled gurgle of water under it, which meant it was not entirely frozen. The fierce cold coming off the ice made him gasp and he was glad of the net socks that gave his feet a little protection.

He walked along the ice road to where it turned North. 'How far does it go, I wonder?' he murmured.

It was not really a question, but Semmel had walked along the bank, too, and she answered. 'The Coldway goes to the edge of the world.'

Zluty did not much like the sound of that, but he only asked, 'How does the device work?'

'We must get the wagon onto the Coldway and you will see,' Flugal said.

'You want to pull the wagon on the ice?' Zluty said uneasily.

'The device can only be used on the Coldway,' Semmel said from the bank. 'It must be fastened to the wagon.'

Zluty had no idea what the device could be or what it would do or how it could make them go faster, but he said he would make a ramp of cold-whites so they could slide the wagon down gently onto the Coldway. Flugal said he need not worry about the ice cracking because it was very thick.

'I am more worried about the hull of the wagon,' Zluty explained.

By the time he had pushed coldwhites from the bank and stamped them into a ramp, the diggers had got the device free, unwrapped it and spread the pieces on the bank beside the wagon. It took all of them and the towropes to ease the wagon down Zluty's ramp onto the ice, then the diggers carried two long flat staves that were part of the device down the ramp and lay them one either side of the wagon. They used the levers that lifted the wagon up so the wheels could be taken on and off, and the diggers pushed the staves under the wagon before lowering it onto them. Finally, Flugal bound the staves to the wheel nubs.

'There,' he said with satisfaction. 'Now the wagon can slide on them instead of on its hull.' He climbed back onto the bank where the other bits of the device lay in a pile of poles and thongs. 'Now for the wings.'

'Wings?' Zluty echoed incredulously.

Flugal did not seem to hear. Indeed, as he began arranging the bits and pieces, Zluty saw the he digger had got the same dreamy look as Semmel had when the memory scents were talking to her. He carefully flattened an area of the coldwhites and began to arrange the poles in a complex pattern. This done, he bound the poles where they crossed with thongs. From time to time, Semmel untied and retied a thong, shifting the joined poles slightly.

Seeing they did not need him, Zluty went to the wagon and heaved the round black fireplate out. He got out the firemoss and a few of the remaining firenuts and started a fire. When it was crackling merrily, he fetched the cooking things and made a thick stew.

As he shaved some of the black mushroom he loved into the pot, he thought of Bily, and glanced across to the mountains, now no more than a black starless mass.

If only he had seen a sign that Bily was safe. At least his brother had been wearing his forage bag, which held his small healing kit, and he had been wearing his cloak, for both were missing. The forage bag would likely contain some food and perhaps the shard of skystone, for which he had whittled a handle so that Bily could use it as a knife or a source of light.

Zluty told himself that a lot could be done with those things, and Bily was resourceful and brave.

Flugal called him and Zluty gave the bubbling stew a final stir before setting the pot to one side and going to find the diggers. They were now laying out great swathes of cloth over the pattern of poles. The wind had begun to gust lightly and this was making it difficult for the diggers to keep the cloth flat and fasten it to the poles. Zluty did his best to help, but there was a great deal of the thin silken material, and it was not easy to hold the material flat so that the diggers could bind it to the poles and then furl it.

When at last all of the cloth was fixed in place and had been furled tightly and bound, Flugal bade Zluty help them raise the whole construction and carry it down to the wagon. They got it upright easily enough, but the wind caught a section of cloth that had not been tied well, and it billowed out, dragging all of them a little distance before they managed to wrestle it to the ground.

That was the moment Zluty began to understand how the device might work. Holding it while the diggers retied the cloth, he felt a thrill of excitement.

In the end, they had to roll the whole thing into a long lumpy bundle to get it down to the wagon, where they could open it out sheltered from the wind by the banks of coldwhites. When it was ready, Zluty held it up, while the diggers attached it bit by bit to the awning frame. It took a long time and Zluty's arms were aching before everything was fastened to the satisfaction of the diggers. They had worked with a silent certainty that convinced him they were being guided by the memory scents.

The stew was cold and lumpy by the time they returned to the bank of the Coldway to eat, but they were all glad of the food. When they had finished, the diggers set aside their bowls and began softly to sing. Zluty quickly realised they were adding the events of the day to the song that would become their telling of the journey. He put away the cooking things, and when the singing was done, he asked Semmel if they would reach the end of the mountains before the Longful Night began.

'The wind will decide,' replied the she digger.

They dragged the wagon along on its staves to where the Coldway turned North, and anchored it using piles of snow. Zluty made very sure the piles were high and he packed them down around the staves to ensure the wagon would not move until they wanted it to. Then the diggers bid Zluty goodnight, for he had said he would wait up until the fire burned out. They climbed down into the wagon, and in a short time, all was silent.

Zluty was tired, too, after the long day, but he felt restless. After the fire went out, he got up and stood on the bank for a time, wrapped in his cloak, watching little clouds of darkness scurrying across the starry sky. Though there were only occasional gusts of wind on the ground, up high it was obviously blowing hard.

He turned to look at the jagged, starless darkness that was the mountain range, wondering where Bily was and what was happening to him. Finally, shivering with cold, Zluty went down the ramp to the ice. He studied the wagon, imagining the wind catching the pieces of cloth once they were unfurled, pulling it along. He was certain he was right about how it would work, but he could not imagine how they were to steer the wagon, or stop it. The Coldway was very straight, but surely the wind would not always blow them obligingly North. And if they could not control the movement of the wagon, they might be blown into one of the banks.

As Zluty lay down in his bedding, the diggers snuggled up beside him for warmth, for it was a good deal colder with the wind coming in. Seeing Semmel was awake, Zluty decided to ask a question that had been nagging at him.

'Did the Makers make the sky crack or find it?'

'One Maker did find it,' Semmel said sleepily.

Zluty felt a surge of disgust. 'Just imagine it,' he said scornfully. 'Finding a crack in the sky and deciding to use it for rubbish. I wonder what happened to make them change their minds and want to come through themselves.'

There was no response, then Zluty heard a soft snoring sound and realised Semmel had fallen asleep.

The snapping of cloth woke Zluty. Opening his eyes, he saw the lengths of rope connecting the various bits of the device were thrumming, which meant there was a strong wind blowing. Zluty was on the verge of going back to sleep when it struck him that if he could see the ropes and the poles, there must be a source of light!

He shed his bedding hastily and crawled out from between the diggers, pulling on his cloak as he came out from under the awning. The wind was icy and blowing hard, so his eyes watered, blinding him. But when he had blinked them clear, Zluty saw what he had known he must see. Hanging just above the horizon, the risen moon shone, enormous and perfectly round. It cast a hard, bright, silvery light over the world, making the coldwhites glitter.

Turning North, Zluty drew in a breath to see the moonlight had turned the Coldway into a shining silver road. He woke the diggers to see and they scrambled up at once, swaddled in their blankets. Zluty pulled his cloak tighter as he watched the diggers take in the moon and Coldway, their faces full of wonder.

'It is a pity the wind is blowing from the wrong direction to use the device, for the moon is so bright it is as good as day,' Zluty said.

'It does not matter which way the wind blows, just so long as it blows,' Flugal said triumphantly, throwing off his blankets and fetching his cloak. 'The device has ways to scoop the wind and throw it where it is goodly for our travelling.'

'You can make the wagon go North along the Coldway, even though the wind is blowing from the East?' Zluty asked doubtfully.

'Must think of the wind as a Makers machine full of sly tricks,' Flugal said as he leapt up onto the frame and began to unfasten tethers. Semmel joined him, running backwards and forwards to unfurl sections of cloth.

'Maybe we ought to wait till it is daylight,' Zluty called up to them. 'Thin ice might not be visible from a distance. Or a crack.'

'It will not matter if the ice is thinly or crackful. So long as we keep moving, we will fly over them,'

Semmel said in her memory scent voice.

The unfurling of the different parts of the cloth, which the diggers called 'wings', was very complex and all of them had to be fixed in the right position before the largest could be unfurled. By the time all was pronounced ready, the wind had got stronger and Flugal had to shout to Zluty to go and kick free the mounds of coldwhites holding the wagon in place.

Semmel called out to him to tie a tether to himself, for the moment it was freed, the wagon would begin to move.

Heart thumping with a mixture of apprehension and excitement, Zluty fastened a towrope about his waist and and then leapt out the door of the wagon. He kicked away the coldwhite anchors, turned at once and scrambled aboard as it began to move.

'It is not a wagon now,' he said to himself. 'It is a vessel.'

The winged vessel slid along the ice on its long staves, gathering speed until it seemed they were truly flying. And though the wind was still blowing from the East, miraculously, they were flying North.

The diggers were perching either side of the vessel at the prow, watchful. Every now and then one of them would suddenly run round the rim and scale the awning frame or one of the long poles sticking up above it to make some change.

Zluty felt guilty that he could do nothing to help. He could only admire the diggers' agility and their mastery of the vessel. He could hardly take his eyes from the billowing, fluttering sails. He had thought they were red because that was the colour of the bags that held them, but once unfurled and seen in daylight, they had proven to be a wonderful golden colour. He marvelled at their terrifying speed, for surely even Redwing had never flown across the land so fast.

But his delight was tempered whenever he looked at the mountains.

'I swear I will find you both, Bily, no matter what it takes,' he whispered.

'Your heart would have the knowing if badness happened to *Bee-lee*,' Semmel said, startling him.

He watched her make another adjustment to the largest wing, and wished he could take comfort from her words. But Bily had been in trouble in the past when they were apart, and he had not always had a feeling about it. Unless Semmel had meant that Zluty would know if Bily had been hurt or *killed*. He shivered at the thought, but some of the sick fear left him, too, because he was sure he *would* know those things, and since he didn't know, Bily must be alive and well.

Bily was dreaming that the egg voice was whispering to him again.

'I chose you because you are small and soft. Large, powerful things do not pay much heed to small soft things. I chose you and your brother because it is your nature to cleave to one another. Only remember that a key that opens a door can also lock it . . .'

When Bily woke, the words of his dream were clear in his mind.

Then he realised he could not move. He could feel rope cutting into him on all sides, even his head and ears, though there was something soft under him. He struggled and then gave a cry of fright when a creature he had never seen before held up a lantern and leaned near to peer into his face.

'Do not be afraid little fluffy thing,' it said in a kindly voice.

Bily saw with a shock that it was a small Monk.

'You hit your head on the mountain,' it went on.

'Will you untie me?' Bily asked, for despite the creature tying him up, it seemed not to mean him any harm.

'You are not tied up,' it said, sounding amused. 'You are in a safesling. Sicklings are carried in them if they are not strong enough to cling and swing. The Great One has been carrying you in it since you fell, but you may ride with me on her back now that you are woken. You will easily fit for you are small enough to be my youngling.'

'Youngling . . .' Bily said, bemused, and realised that this Monk was a *she Monk*.

17

'I am Seshla,' said the she Monk.

'I . . . my name is Bily,' Bily stammered. 'I did not know there were any she Monks. I thought he Monks came from metal eggs like me and my brother, Zluty.'

Seshla did not seem surprised at his words, but her dark eyes grew suddenly sad. 'You speak of the lostlings – the he Monks of Stonehouse who are our brothers and sons and fathers, though they have no memory of us.'

'I don't understand,' Bily said.

'In obedience to the Makers plan, we surrender

almost all he Monk younglings to their service, but their memories of us might unsettle them, so they must be taken from them.'

'Because their sadness would muddle the Makers metal, and then they might refuse to do the things the Makers want them to do . . .' Bily murmured, wondering if the Makers had found out that emotions affected the power of their metal.

Seshla tilted her head and gave him a bright, interested look. 'That is true. The Makers do not trust she Monks because our metal is unawakened so that we can bear younglings. We could not do that if our metal was bound. They need us to bear younglings, but they fear our influence over the he Monks, so we must be hidden away and forgotten.'

Bily tried to sit up in the safesling and discovered with a sick lurch of his stomach that he was suspended over a sheer drop. He could not see what lay below because of the mist, and it was the same when he looked up.

'Where is the Monster?' he asked with sudden alarm.

'Monster?' Seshla said, then her eyes widened. 'Ah, that is how you name the Changebringer. The Great One is watching over him.'

'The Changebringer?' Bily echoed. 'The Great One?'

'Wait,' said Seshla, and climbed up out of sight, taking her lantern and leaving Bily dangling in darkness. A moment later, the rope sling gave a jerk and she was hauling him onto a ledge covered in cold fluffs. There was a dark cave open in the side of the mountain, and he could just see the Monster stretched out asleep by the light of the lantern.

The Monster was not moving and Bily's heart began to pound with alarm. He fought to get free of the net, until Seshla bid him be still and used her long deft fingers to free him.

As soon as the rope sling fell away, Bily crawled into the cave. He stroked the Monster's tufted ears and kissed its nose, but it did not stir, nor could he reach its mind.

Frightened, he laid his cheek against its flank and listened. With relief, he felt its heart beating steadily and strongly, though rather too slowly. But it was hot, too, which was a good sign. He examined its body as best he was able, but could find no injury. Was it possible there was something wrong inside it because of the way the Nightbeast had carried it? Or was its metal beginning to sicken again now that the potion was wearing off?

'What are you?' asked a great breathy voice in his mind.

Even before he lifted his head, Bily realised that what he had thought to be the immense darkness of the cave was the Nightbeast. His knees trembled as he looked up into its narrowed, gleaming green eyes.

'Its name is Bily, Great One,' Seshla said, coming to sit beside Bily and wrapping something thick and soft around his shoulders. 'You are a he, aren't you?' she whispered to Bily.

Bily nodded, unable to find his voice.

'Why did you capture us?' he managed to ask at last, though his voice sounded small and rather shaky.

'The wise ones sent me to find the broken Listener they call Changebringer,' the Nightbeast said in its vast sighing voice. Like the Monster and the Cloud Monster it spoke aloud at the same time as inside his mind. 'The Listeners gave me his scent in a dream and that is how I tracked him. I smelled you clinging to him, little Softling, but I thought you were his rider as Seshla is mine.'

Bily was shocked that the Nightbeast spoke of the Monster as a He, but the diggers in the encampment had done the same, and he had resolved to try to follow their customs.

'What will you do with us?' he finally asked, tremulously.

The green eyes flashed with amusement. 'I do not propose to do anything with you or to you, for I did not bring *you*. You brought yourself.'

'I could not just let you take the Monster,' Bily said softly. 'It . . . he is sick, you see. I have been looking after him.'

The eyes narrowed. 'Do you serve him out of love, or because you fear the anger of the Listeners or the wrath of the Makers?'

'I just wanted to help the Monster,' Bily said. Then he added truthfully. 'I *was* afraid of it . . .him to begin with, but he was in such pain, and after a while we became friends.'

There was a pause during which those enormous green eyes seemed to look through Bily's skin and bone. 'Then it is as I supposed when I scented you – you are a true rider.'

Bily said, startled, 'I don't *ride* the Monster.' He had ridden on the Cloud Monster. But that had been an emergency.

'A rider is not only one who rides. It means one who shares a mutual bond with another, and where each of them carries the other in their heart as a beloved burden,' Seshla said. 'The Great One is saying that you share the same bond of love with the Changebringer as I share with *her*.' She paused. 'You smell hungry.' She turned to rummage in a bag she carried over her shoulder and chest, just as he carried his forage bag. Then she crowed with triumph and handed Bily a round, heavy, slightly greasy lump that smelled sweet. She took out another lump and bit into it.

Realising all at once how dreadfully hungry he was, Bily nibbled gingerly at his lump. It was like bread dough that had not been cooked, and it was terribly sweet, but he was grateful to be eating anything.

Seshla finished her lump and rummaged again in her bag, this time producing a gourd of water, from which Bily drank thankfully, when she offered it.

'What about the Nightbeast?' he asked, returning the gourd to her.

The she Monk showed her teeth to the Nightbeast in a rather ferocious grin, and made a chittering noise, before looking back at Bily.

'That is a fine name for her, but you need not worry about her being hungry. She ate well in preparation for this journey. She will only slake her thirst with snow before we go on.'

Snow, Bily thought. That was the word the Makers used for cold fluffs.

'The Changebringer is broken,' Seshla went on,

glancing at the Monster's sleeping face. 'I doubt he could carry you.'

'He couldn't,' Bily agreed, though he did not like to hear her say the Monster was broken. 'He can't walk. That is why we were pulling him in the wagon. We were trying to bring it . . . him to the Velvet City where he can be healed.'

The Nightbeast gave a low rumbling growl. 'That healing would come at a high price. And the wise ones say your Monster has no wish to return to the Velvet City.'

'I don't know how they can know that. But he must go back, else die,' Bily said. Then he hesitated. 'But isn't that where *you* mean to take him?'

'I will carry him to the wise ones in the Hidden Place,' the Nightbeast said, rather haughtily.

'But who are the wise ones?' Bily asked.

'They are very old she Monks. They will take care of the Changebringer and instruct him, if he will listen,' Seshla said.

Instruct him in what? Bily wondered.

But before he could ask, the Nightbeast rose in one huge soft movement, almost invisible against the darkness. Bily saw again the flash of the metal about its neck, and wanted to ask about it, but

Seshla was standing up, too.

'It is time to go,' she told him.

'You may go with us, Softling, if you wish,' the Nightbeast said, again speaking inside Bily's head.

'I will go with the Monster,' Bily said firmly.

Seshla gave the little bobbing nod that seemed to mean something more than merely agreement. 'The wise ones will be curious about you. Not one of them has foreseen you.'

'Probably because I don't have Makers metal in me,' Bily murmured.

'Though you are small, you cannot have come through the sky crack by chance, and no one could survive that journey without Makers metal in them,' Seshla said. 'Your metal must be unawakened like mine or damaged like the Great One's.'

Bily looked at the Nightbeast. 'Your metal is damaged?'

'The Makers sent me through the sky crack as a cub to serve as a guard of the borders of the Hidden Place, to keep the she Monks imprisoned there,' the Nightbeast said. 'My metal was supposed to awaken and bind me to the Makers machines as soon as I was within the ice peaks surrounding the Hidden Place, but it did not bind.

Being a cub, I knew nothing and near died of cold and hunger, wandering near the Long Pool in the end days of Winter. But the world's dream came and the she Monks found me by its light. When they understood what had happened, they bade me patrol the perimeter so that the Makers would believe I was bound to their metal, for Makers hate things that do not work as they are meant to. They might be puzzled that they could not track me, but as long as I did what I was meant to do, they would think the fault was a small one. They would never know I was not bound to their metal. And that is how it came that the she Monks are not truly imprisoned.'

Seshla gave Bily a glimmering, wicked wink, then she said more seriously, 'I did not come through the sky crack. I was born here of a she Monk, as was my mother and *her* mother before her. My brothers, too, though they do not remember it once they leave the Hidden Place. I have Makers metal inside me, as do all younglings born of those with Makers metal. But because I am a she Monk, my metal was never woken.'

'It was not woken so you could have younglings,' Bily remembered.

'Exactly. But because I am not bound, I do not have to follow the Makers plan. I chose not to have any younglings so that I could serve as first rider to the Great One. The Makers do not know this. If they did, I would not be allowed to live, for our ability to bear younglings is the sole value of a she Monk to the Makers.'

Seshla rose and stretched her long furred arms.

'In the beginning, a Makers metal barrier kept us imprisoned. The Hidden Place cannot be seen by the world and we could not venture beyond its icy borders, save when we came to the mainland to tithe. The Makers controlled the metal barrier and watched us closely to be sure all the she Monks that went out also returned. But over time, she Monks disappeared. Most likely they perished, but it alarmed the Makers, and that is why they sent the Great One to guard us and prevent any other creature coming near the Hidden Place. Instead, our prison has became a secret refuge.'

Bily thought there were gaps in the she Monk's telling, and he said, 'She Listeners have young-lings, even though they are not bound to Makers machines.'

'They are a different kind from Monks, as are

you and I, little Softling,' the Nightbeast said.

'Listener's metal is bound to a Makers machine,' Seshla said. 'But theirs is a very subtle binding made to hold the minds in thrall, rather than the body. It does not affect their metal – unless a Listener transgresses in some way. Such as going far from the Velvet City. The binding will then kill the Listener slowly, so that they will die without knowing why.'

'And if they come to understand that they will die if they do not return to the Velvet City?' Bily asked anxiously.

'I think the Makers would not want such a Listener to return to the Velvet city,' Seshla said, and gave the Monster a thoughtful look. 'But if they went back, I think the metal would cease sickening.'

Bily longed to ask what the wise ones wanted with the Monster, but instead he asked, 'Where is the Hidden Place?'

'Northmost,' Seshla said. 'It is the hot secret heart of the ice maze. Soon you will see it. Now, will you ride with me on the back of the Great One, or be carried in the safesling?'

'I would ride,' Bily said, with a stab of anguish

that again he would be going where Zluty could not follow. The she Monk must have felt his hesitation, for she merely continued to look at him expectantly.

'It is my brother, Zluty,' he explained. 'The Nightbeast took me from him and our digger friends and they will be frantic with worry for us. If only I could let them know we are safe.'

'I know the longing for a brotherblood,' Seshla said sadly. She considered and then clapped her big soft hands. 'Once I have brought you and the Changebringer to the wise ones, the Great One and I will travel back to seek out your brother and his companions. We will let them know you are safe and bring them to you, if they desire it.'

'Oh, that would be wonderful,' Bily cried. He looked at the Monster, who lay unmoving, and frowned. 'Why doesn't it . . . he wake? Is it his metal sickening?'

'His metal *is* sickening, Softling, but the Changebringer sleeps because I bit him using a venom that would calm him, so he would not struggle and hurt himself,' said the Nightbeast. 'He is not truly sleeping, but lost in memories, yet he will wake as from a dream.'

Bily reached out with helpless love to stroke the Monster's paw, wanting to say something about how much it had slept and how ill it had been, but the Nightbeast was moving like a great soft dark shadow to the mouth of the cave. It struck Bily that despite her immense size, the Nightbeast was similar in kind to the Monster, with her pointed ears and long tail.

'The sleep bestowed by the Great One will not harm your Monster,' Seshla said. She patted Bily's head kindly, then ran out of the cave on all fours and leapt without hesitation onto the Nightbeast's mane. Catching two great handfuls of fur, she climbed up onto her broad back, then she lowered her long tail to Bily. He took hold of it gingerly.

'Hold tight,' Seshla said, and lifted him without difficulty to sit behind her. Bily wrapped his arms about her middle and felt the wiry strength of her under her soft pelt, as she leaned forward against the Nightbeast's neck.

The Nightbeast bent her head to lap at the cold fluffs piled up on the ledge. When she had had her fill, she reached into the cave to take up the Monster in her jaws and set off once more along the narrow ledge.

18

Bily tried hard not to think about how narrow the ledge was.

'You need not squash the life out of me to prove how strong you are,' Seshla protested, smiling over her shoulder at Bily to show she was joking.

Embarrassed, Bily loosened his grip and tried to relax.

It was certainly more comfortable riding on the Nightbeast's wide warm back than clinging precariously to the Monster's leg.

The wind gusted icily, but at least it cleared

away the clouds, and for the first time Bily could see the stars. He looked down, desperate to see fire or a flash of the red awning that would tell him Zluty was heading North, too, but the thick grey mist made it impossible to see anything.

As the night wore on, the wind pushed the cloud away and thinned the mist, and when day dawned, Bily finally saw the sky. It was the palest blue, and under it the vast white land stretched from the mountains to the Eastern horizon. But there was no sign of the wagon, nor of a fire.

There were rocky black outcrops here and there, however, as well as hillocks that could conceal buried Maker devices big enough to block his view of the wagon. And Zluty would not have wanted to waste time lighting a fire when there were so few firenuts left. It was still very early so Zluty and the others were probably sleeping. Or was it possible that Zluty had decided to turn back? Somehow, Bily could not believe that.

He did not know how long Zluty and the diggers had been gone before the Nightbeast had torn open the awning, but it was strange that no one had cried out at the sight of the Nightbeast.

They must have ventured further from the wagon than they had intended.

He was about to ask Seshla if she had seen them, when he caught sight of something out of the corner of his eye down on the plain. He turned his head to look and caught his breath at the sight of a great golden bird skimming over a silver-grey river running North.

'Hold tight,' Seshla cried.

Bily obeyed as he looked over her shoulder. He gasped to find that the Nightbeast was approaching the wide mouth of a dark hole in the mountain side where the ledge path had collapsed. He could see where the ledge ran on the other side of the hole, but the hole itself was enormous. The Nightbeast stopped on the edge of it and its muscles bunched.

With a surge of terror, Bily understood that it was going to leap over the hole.

Seshla must have felt his fear, for she sent words straight to his mind.

'Do not be afraid, Bily. The Great One has eyes that can see in the dark.'

And without warning, the Nightbeast leapt *into the hole*.

Nothing had ever frightened Bily more than that great falling leap into utter darkness. He was so stiff with terror that if Seshla's tail had not snaked around his waist, he would have tumbled from the Nightbeast when it landed hard.

Then it leapt again and again.

'Hold very tight, now,' Seshla said and Bily obeyed, but this time, instead of springing forward again, the Nightbeast began to slide down. As they picked up speed, the air whipping past his ears grew icy cold and Bily huddled behind the she Monk, eyes squeezed closed, certain he would die of cold if he did not die of fear.

They seemed to slide into the chilly dark for hours, and Bily grew colder than he had ever been in his life. He could no longer feel his toes or his fingers, and fear had faded into a kind of numbness, by the time he saw light through his eyelids. He thought he was dreaming, but when he opened his eyes he saw a dim greenish light ahead. It reminded him of being under the water in the flooded cellar.

Seshla had flattened herself against the neck of the Nightbeast, so Bily had only to lift his head to see over her. He forgot his fear in wonder, for the light grew enough to see that they were sliding along a steep slanting tunnel of greenish ice. There were holes in the sides and overhead and he was astonished to see a little dark face look out fleetingly, its eyes shining and red.

As the light strengthened, he realised they were getting closer to the source. Finally the ice tunnel opened into a great chasm, then they were gliding over the surface of a frozen lake!

Looking up, Bily saw the light flowing into the chasm was daylight turned greenish as it reflected off the ice. His hands and fur had a greenish tinge, too, as did Seshla's pelt. Even the Nightbeast's pelt looked green.

They were going more slowly now, and Bily dared to sit up properly and look as the Nightbeast glided silently along the glittering passage.

'We are nearing the end of the Mountains,' Seshla said, her voice turned strange and hollow. 'Soon we will come to the Coldway and that will bring us to the ice maze.'

Bily's heart leapt, for surely Semmel had spoken of the Coldway. But they had travelled so fast on the back of the Nightbeast, that even if Zluty and the diggers had continued North, it would be many days before they reached the Coldway.

He comforted himself with Seshla's promise that she and the Nightbeast would seek Zluty out once he and the Monster had been delivered to the wise ones.

Bily noticed that the greenish light was fading. He looked up to see the sky was clear but darkening. He thought he saw a star. 'Has night come already?' he asked.

'Not quite, but soon the last day will end,' Seshla replied.

'Last day?' Bily asked.

'Before the Long Night comes,' Seshla said. 'But do not fear, we will be in the Hidden Place before the first ice blizzard comes.'

'*Ice* blizzard?' Bily said. 'I thought they only happened in the mountains?'

'In the South, the ice blizzards happen only in the mountains, but in the North once the Long Night begins, they leap down to ravage the land. No one can travel during the worst ice blizzards, not even the Great One.'

Bily thought in anguish of Zluty and the diggers. They were coming North, straight into the ice blizzards!

———————

Zluty felt that he was flying, they were now moving so swiftly along the Coldway.

The wind had shifted and was now behind them, so that there was little the diggers had to do. Zluty looked around him and thought a vessel deserved a name, especially one that had carried them so faithfully and so far.

He asked the diggers if they could think of a good name, but they were too absorbed in the memory scents helping them to manage the vessel. It made Zluty feel lonely and miss Bily more than ever.

He looked over at the mountains which had become taller and much more jagged than those further South. He could not see any movement, but he had not truly expected to see anything. He turned East and felt a prickle of unease, for threatening clouds gathered on the Eastern horizon, stretching out long black fingers towards him.

He wondered if a storm was brewing. If so, they would need to get the vessel off the Coldway. The safest place to anchor it would be one of the large mounds of snow they had passed from time to time. That would offer some protection. He wondered how difficult it would be to remove the vessel's wings and lay them flat on the ground.

He longed to suggest they stop, but aside from wanting to go on as fast as possible, he was afraid that Semmel would say they did not yet know how to stop. So he kept a close eye on the clouds and prayed they would reach the end of the mountains before the storm came, and that by then the diggers might have learned how to stop and where to find shelter.

They flew on and Zluty felt restless with nothing to do save watch the world rushing by. He decided to make a meal. He could not light a fire, so he rummaged in sacks and bundles to assemble a meal from the little that remained of their supplies.

When he called the diggers to come and eat, he half expected them to scorn his humble muddle of bits and pieces, but Flugal leapt down eagerly to scoop up some nuts and dried fruit and a bit of bread spread with leftover stew before carrying his food with him back to the rim of the vessel. Then it was Semmel's turn, and she praised him for his cleverness in preparing a meal they could eat while they tended the vessel.

Pleased, Zluty brought his own food up to the

front of the vessel where the diggers had settled themselves, and sat cross-legged on the bale of sweetgrass to eat it so that he could see out.

After he had finished, he found himself weaving into a song all the sounds of their journey – the sharp swishing scrape of the staves over the rough ice of the Coldway, the flutter and snap of different bits of the wing structure, the creak of a towrope whenever the diggers untied a rope and adjusted the wings, and occasionally, the sharp ting of metal when the little rings holding bits of cloth together struck the metal awning frame.

The song he was making and the fluttering golden wing device gave him the perfect idea of a name for the vessel. They could call it *Goldsong.*

He started violently when Semmel lay a paw on his arm. Instead of speaking, she pointed, and he turned to see that the black cloud had come forward in a dark wave, blotting out all the sky, save for a small patch of dark blue ahead of them, where a scattering of stars shone.

'We must stop soonly,' Semmel said.

'Stop how?' Zluty asked.

'We will turn the smaller parts of the wings to catch the air and throw it into the biggest part

from the front,' Flugal called from the awning overhead. 'That will stop the vessel, but I must do it with carefulness so we do not turn suddenly and go into the bank.'

A chill ran through Zluty at the thought, for the bank was now a good deal higher than it had been, and frozen solid. If they hit it going so fast, the vessel would crack open.

He was about to shout out to the diggers that they had better slow the vessel down, for the wind was getting stronger by the second, but when he glanced North, he was thrilled to see the end of the range! He hastened to the front of the vessel and looked out eagerly. He had not been mistaken. The end of the range was still a good way off, but at the speed they were doing they would cover the distance quickly. He looked back at the dark cloud swallowing the sky behind them, and wondered if they might be going fast enough to beat the blizzard.

Even as this thought came to him, Flugal shouted that they must stop the vessel. Zluty turned and watched, heart in his mouth, as Semmel and her mate wove their complex and effortless dance about one another, running lightly up and down the towropes, lowering or adjusting sections of the wings. At last the diggers spilled air into the great sail. There was a great snap of cloth and a slight jerk, then the vessel slowed swiftly, sliding to a smooth halt alongside the bank next to a great mound of coldwhites.

'Push the vessel against the bank and anchor the staves,' Flugal signalled Zluty, for it was hard to hear anything now over the howling wind.

Zluty did not waste time asking questions. He was still wearing his net socks and he leapt out of the vessel onto the ice and shoved it hard against the bank, then he began gouging up armfuls of coldwhites and pushing them over and behind the staves. When Semmel called him to come and help bring down the big poles, he saw they could be laid down flat along the length of the vessel without removing them. But the heavy rigging that held the largest wing section had tangled around the awning frame, and with the wind pulling at it, it proved impossible to free.

'Leave it,' Zluty shouted, for coldwhites were beginning to fill the air. 'Untie the end and let the cloth flap. That way it can't catch the wind and pull the vessel free.'

Flugal obeyed, giving the wildly flapping piece of wing cloth an anguished look, while Zluty pushed the side of the frame out so that it rested on the mound of coldwhites. Then he climbed onto it, unrolled the torn awning over it and tied it down. Finally, he jumped onto the mound to push stakes deep into it so that he could use the towropes to hold the awning flat.

By the time he had secured the awning and carried the bee urn and the moss balls down under it, Semmel and Flugal were burrowing into the side of the mound, creating a cave. It was well done, for outside, nothing at all could be seen now but the flying coldwhites that caught the light of the lantern Semmel had lit.

The diggers pushed blankets into the cave, turning it into a nest just large enough for them all to fit, and once they were in it, Zluty pulled a ground sheet up to block the opening. It was not a moment too soon, for just as he pushed in the last peg, a long shuddering roar shook the air, then coldwhites began striking the awning with such violent force that Zluty was glad the diggers had made a cave, for the awning might well collapse under such an onslaught.

'The wind is blowing the coldwhites very hard,' he shouted to Semmel.

'They are not coldwhites, *Zchloo-tee*,' she signalled gravely. 'They are *ice flowers*.'

Only then did Zluty understand. The storm was not a blizzard – it was an *ice blizzard*.

Semmel nodded as if he had spoken his thought aloud, and said, 'The Longful Night has begun.'

three

THE
LONGFUL
NIGHT

19

The Nightbeast glided from the mouth of the ice chasm into the open, and Bily saw that although they had reached the end of the stony black mountain range, ahead were more mountains covered in cold fluffs and rising up in great separate spikes against the dark blue sky, like the ghosts of mountains. Through the gaps between them, he could see two bright stars like mismatched eyes, just above the horizon, and realised it was verging on night.

The land beyond the white mountains stretched out flat and utterly featureless, save for the grey river that flowed past the mouth of the ice chasm, before turning to trace the inner curve of the arc of white peaks. Then it disappeared out of sight around the farthest peak.

Instead of racing North through the gap between the two ice peaks directly ahead, as Bily expected her to do, the Nightbeast ran at an angle that brought her to the bank of the river where it curved back on itself.

His heart juddered when the Nightbeast stopped to gather herself, fearing she would leap over it, but instead, she leapt into it.

At the last minute, Bily saw that the river was frozen! The ice was so thick that it did not even creak when they landed.

Once again the Nightbeast was gliding forward on her great soft paws, but this time she began to lope in a low, rocking movement that was part running and part gliding. As they passed the first of the white mountains, Bily was astonished to see that it was not a mountain at all but a great peak of ice. When they were passing the second ice peak, a thought struck him.

'Seshla, is this the Coldway?' he asked, gesturing to the ice river under them.

The she Monk looked back over her shoulder at him, her dark eyes sparkling. 'Yes!' she said, the word coming out in a puff of cloud. 'It will bring us to the place where we must enter the ice maze.' Her eyes looked past him and became wary. 'Hold tight, Bily. We must go very fast now.'

As she bent over the Nightbeast's neck, her pace increased. Bily bent low, too, but he could not resist looking back over his shoulder to see what Seshla had seen. His breath caught in his throat at the sight of a great black wave of cloud rapidly moving North towards them. He could see nothing of the land under it save a dim roil of smudged grey, and he knew at once what it was.

Ice blizzard! he whispered, and his fear for himself gave way to a far greater fear for Zluty and the diggers, for they had surely been overtaken it.

The Nightbeast was moving so swiftly that by the time Bily turned back to face the front, they were approaching the last ice peak. The moment they were clear of it, he saw that the Coldway turned to run straight North again.

Only then, as they raced towards the end of the Coldway, did Bily understand that the land truly did end. Beyond lay a black sea upon which floated pieces of ice. It ran as far as he could see and in the distance there were clusters of ice peaks rising up from it. The farthest was shrouded in mist.

It was to this cluster of ice peaks that Seshla now pointed, as the Nightbeast came to a stop at the end of the Coldway. 'There is the Hidden Place,' the she Monk announced.

'Why is there so much mist around it?' Bily asked, wondering if it was something the Makers had conjured.

'The other peaks are merely floating mountains of ice, but the Hidden Place is a true island of stone, rooted in the earth, and surrounded by a ring of ice peaks,' the she Monk said as the Nightbeast leapt from the ice river up onto the bank.

It was not really an answer, but before he could say so, Seshla turned and clasped her long strong arm about Bily's waist. Lifting him like he weighed no more than a digger, she swung herself down to the ground, using only one hand and her clever hand-like feet.

When she set him down, Bily saw that she was gazing South, transfixed, and he turned to look. He had hoped with all of his heart to see the wagon with its red awning, but there was

only the wave of black clouds closer than ever.

'It is unusual for an ice blizzard to come at the very beginning of the Long Night,' Seshla murmured, sounding troubled. 'I do not like it. But have no fear, we will be safe among my people before it reaches us.'

'But . . . Zluty . . . the diggers . . .' Bily stammered. He was so distressed that his voice failed him.

'The ice blizzard that comes is only a youngling. It will not last long, and you have said that your brother is sensible and brave,' Seshla said. 'He and his companions will have found shelter.'

Her words calmed Bily, because Zluty *was* brave and very resourceful. And the diggers had the memory scents to help them. Even so, Bily wished he had seen some sign of the wagon from the mountains.

'Now we must cross the ice maze,' Seshla said.

But Bily hardly heard her, for he was gaping up at the enormous Nightbeast, which he now saw properly for the first time. She *was* shaped like the Monster, whom she had gently deposited on the cold fluffs. She was much bigger and less finely made, though maybe much of her rough bulk was her fur, for it was very thick, especially the great mane about her neck and face. The strangest thing was that her pelt was not black but pure white, and yet her pelt *had* been black, he was sure of it. Had he not named her Nightbeast because of her midnight pelt? Then he remembered it had looked quite green when they had been in the ice chasm.

'Your fur changes colour!' he cried.

'It does,' Seshla said crossly. 'It is very annoying when we play hiding games because the Great One always turns the colour of her surroundings.' She turned to say a rather formal sounding farewell to the Nightbeast.

'Isn't she coming with us?' Bily asked, confused.

'She will swim to the Hidden Place, for this early in Winter the ice is too thin to bear her weight,' Seshla said. 'There is an open passage through the ice floes further to the West, which she always swims along, to keep it open. As the Long Night deepens, the sea ice will freeze into a solid sheet and an open passage means the small swimming beasts can rise to get air without having to go far out from the mainland; and those that live on land can forage in the water to feed themselves. But for us the way to the Hidden Place is by means of the ice maze.'

'You mean . . .' Bily began, then stopped.

'We must leap and creep and jump across the floes,' Seshla said, almost playfully. But then her bright eyes grew serious. 'It is not an easy passage, Bily, but we must go now. Once the ice blizzard reaches us, the passage will be truly perilous because the floes will shift and bump against one another, and we will not be able to carry the Listener across them.'

As she spoke, she was removing several long thin poles that had been tucked under the metal about the Nightbeast's neck and chest. In no time she had fitted them end to end, until she had two very long poles. She pulled the safesling from her bag and threaded it between the poles, then she drew out from her bag the soft thick rug that she had put around his shoulders, and pressed it into the safesling to make a mattress. Finally, she lashed the two ends of the poles together.

'This is a travois,' she said, and stepped back as the Nightbeast again closed her teeth on the Monster's nape and lifted him gently into it.

The she Monk pulled the sides of the net up so that the Monster was securely cradled, saying, 'The rug under the Changebringer is made of the

Great One's combings, which are waterproof. It will keep the Listener dry if water splashes. Fortunately, his body is very warm so he will not get cold.'

'But how can we get the travois out there?' Bily asked, gesturing to the Hidden Place in its misty shroud.

'I will drag it. The long poles will straddle the gaps between the ice floes and distribute the weight of the Listener,' Seshla said. She looked

into Bily's face. 'I could carry you both in it, but it will be better – safer – if you can run on your own feet. The ice floes move constantly and you must always step as close to the centre as possible, lest it tip under your weight. Once you get the trick of it, you will find it is not so hard.' She gave him an encouraging look, but Bily could not muster a smile for her.

She cocked her head and studied him for a moment, sniffing, then she gave a laugh and patted his head. 'After all, I think it will be better if you ride with the Listener, Bily. You do not weigh more than a snowflake, and you must not fall into the water, for it is deadly cold. Even if you should survive the cold, the ice floe would right itself and, if it was too close to the next one, I would not be able to reach you.'

Bily was trembling from head to toe, but then he felt a hot wind. He turned to find the Nightbeast had brought her enormous head down to his level and was warming him with a long, sweet breath. He heard her words in his mind.

'Little Softling, if your brother is so brave, you must be brave, too, for does not the same blood run through you both?'

Bily knew he was not brave like Zluty, but the Nightbeast's words reminded him that since they had left the cottage he had done many things that had frightened him, and he knew he could not let his fears master him now. He gulped back a sob and took a deep shuddering breath. Then he turned to Seshla.

'I will not ride. I will walk beside you.' His voice came out in a whisper, but Seshla merely nodded and turned to take up the bound end of the travois poles.

'Follow and go where I go,' she said. 'Take your time and step as far onto each floe as you can. If you slip, throw yourself to the centre, spread your arms and legs wide and lie flat and still until it settles. Think only of the floe under you and then of the next one.'

Bily nodded, but as Seshla turned North he could not help casting one final look back to see that the dark reaching fingers of the ice blizzard had almost closed over the sky now.

When he turned North again, the Nightbeast had vanished, her paw prints running West along the edge of the land.

20

For what seemed like days, the ice blizzard lashed the shelter stretched between the vessel and the mound of coldwhites. The awning collapsed and a great coldwhite mound slid over the opening of the ice cave. Fortunately, the ground sheet held and, after digging a small hole so that air could get in, the diggers had deepened the cave to give them more room.

Flugal discovered the mound of coldwhites covered another Makers device, but even he knew it was not the moment to excavate it.

They cuddled close to one another under all the

blankets and cloaks, and curled around the bee urn and the soft constant warmth of the moss balls. It was impossible to speak because of the screaming of the ice blizzard, and finally, they slept.

Zluty dreamed of the egg voice.

'Perhaps I am foolish to rely upon two small beings to save a world,' it said softly. 'It would be better to create one strong creature, and bind it to my will. But that is the old hard way. Better to put my faith in the heart binding of these little brothers, for it will take both of them . . .'

'Wake, Zluty!'

Zluty opened his eyes, the egg voice fading in his mind. He was not confused. He knew where he was and why, but it was utterly dark inside the coldwhite cave. The lantern must have gone out.

He sat up, head aching from the bad air, but almost at once, cold fresh air blew onto his face. He turned his mouth to it and breathed deeply.

'Zluty!' Flugal said again.

'I am awake,' Zluty said. 'The ice blizzard . . .'

'It is over,' said Semmel. There a little scratching noise and then the lantern flared in her paws. 'We are luckful that it was not a bad ice blizzard, *Zchloo-tee*.'

Zluty thought she must be making a joke.

'We dug a little hole to make sure the ice blizzard was over,' Flugal said. 'You cannot see, for it is very darkful now the Longful Night has come. But we must get out of here and go on fastly, for we dare not be out in the open if a proper ice blizzard comes.'

'A *proper* ice blizzard,' Zluty muttered, then remembered with a jolt of excitement that he had seen the end of the mountains. He levered himself to his knees and helped the diggers to make an opening big enough for them to crawl out, and then he widened the hole and passed out everything to them, before crawling out himself.

The lantern's light seemed small and frail as a candle flame in the vast blackness that surrounded them.

Zluty took it and went to see how the vessel had fared. The ice that had fallen had formed a thick, brittle crust over the coldwhites that crunched under his feet. Ice had fallen on the Coldway, too, so that it was now as white as the ground either side and he would not have known it was there at all but for its steep banks. The vessel was completely white.

Setting the lantern down, Zluty slithered down onto the Coldway carrying the bee urns and the firemoss balls. Hauling open the door with a great crunching sound, he climbed inside the vessel and set his burdens down. He was startled to see feathers of ice had formed all along the awning frame, and every rope had its own little beard of ice. Then the diggers scrambled onto the vessel.

Flugal uttered a cry of dismay and Zluty turned to see that he was looking at the large bit of wing cloth they had left flapping. It had been torn to tatters and the pole it was attached to had also broken.

'It cannot be mended,' Semmel said.

'We can still use the other parts of the wings,' Flugal said. 'We will not be able to go very fastly, but it will be quicker than dragging the vessel along by the towropes.'

It took them a good deal longer than any of them liked to scrape the worst of the ice from the inside of the vessel and from the towropes and wing cloth, and to raise the intact pole and fix it in place.

It was bone-achingly cold and the wind was growing stronger again. Zluty shivered as he worked, despite wearing his cape with the hood up. Only when he was labouring to hack away the now solid coldwhite anchors on the Coldway, did he feel warm. He longed for a fire, but they had to get moving, for the lack of stars told him the sky was still full of cloud, and the rising wind hinted ominously at another ice blizzard.

When they were finally ready, Semmel gave him the lantern and bade him hang it on the end of the broken pole so that it stuck out the front of the vessel.

'It will give us some lightfulness so we can see if the Coldway is cracked,' she said.

Zluty did as she bid and when Flugal commanded it, Zluty kicked away the last of the coldwhite anchors and used the towropes to haul the vessel's nose free from the bank in a great crackling of ice. Once he had got the vessel into the middle of the Coldway, the diggers raised the smaller wing cloths. The vessel lurched forward with a great crunching of ice, and Zluty made haste to get back on. He went to stand by the bee urn, and pressed his cold fingers around the moss balls, waiting for them to thaw as the diggers unfurled the largest of the remaining wing cloths.

Even as they tied it quickly in place, it billowed out and filled with wind. The vessel gave another crunching lurch and then moved slowly forward with a great screeching that made Zluty's fur fluff up. It was the sound the staves were making, running over the rime of ice that had formed on the Coldway.

Watching the diggers adjust the smaller sails until the vessel was moving faster, Zluty realised he was beginning to understand how the wings worked. Given time, he would be able to work them himself.

He noticed Flugal cast a last regretful glance back at the mound, where he had not had the chance to look at the Maker device within it, and despite everything, Zluty smiled.

He turned to look at the mountains but it was still too dark to make them out. Fortunately they did not need them for guidance, because the Coldway ran North. And even if it had not done so, his own senses had got their bearings now that the ice blizzard was over.

The wind gradually shifted until it was blowing

from behind them and the vessel went more steadily. The Coldway ran so straight that after a time Semmel suggested they eat. Before Zluty could think what there was left, the she digger darted to her little pack and brought out a small sweet-scented pouch of what looked to be damp grains.

'We can sprinkle it on porridge. It will make us strongful.'

'I would love to make hot porridge but we can't light a fire in the vessel when it is moving,' Zluty reminded her regretfully. The mere thought of porridge made his stomach rumble, but it also gave his heart a twinge, because that was what Bily had always cooked for him the morning before he set out on his trips to the Northern Forest.

'You can light a small fire,' Semmel said, to his surprise. She pointed to the wet deck where the ice they had not been able to scrape off had turned to slush. 'When there is so much wet iciness we will be safely even if the fire spills.'

Zluty needed no more encouragement, and even though the porridge that finally resulted from his unsteady cooking was burnt in some parts and raw in others, it was delicious. The stuff Semmel had given him to sprinkle on it was lovely but also strangely familiar. He questioned her about it when she sat with him by the fire to eat, leaving Flugal to watch the sails. She told him the diggers got the stuff from trees growing inside a crevice in the white desert. When she described the manner of gathering it, he found it was exactly the same as when he tapped trees in the Northern Forest for sap. But instead of keeping the thick sweet liquid in stoppered urns, the diggers dried it to a crunchy sweetness so they could carry it in pouches.

'Did you learn anything else from the memory scents?' Zluty asked.

'I have the knowing of a chasm made of ice where the vessel can go to be safe, *Zchloo-tee*,' she said. 'I do not yet have the knowing about food, but there is fresh water in the ice chasm and that will be important because the water of the Edgeless Sea cannot be drunk.'

'Why not?' Zluty asked.

'I do not have that knowing,' Semmel said. 'There is something about it in the scent memories but . . .' She gave the little tail twitch that served as a shrug.

'It is a great mystery that the rebel diggers brought back scent memories about the North, yet chose to make it so they cannot be unlocked,' Flugal said. 'And why did they keep no memory in themselves? I am hungry for knowing the why of that.'

'How did the diggers know to make sure the scent memories could not be unlocked?' Zluty asked.

'They kept some memories,' Semmel told them. 'They kept the knowing of the digger camp and how to return there.'

'It can't be a Makers machine that took their memories,' Zluty said. 'That would have taken them all.' He was thinking of the enormous machine in Stonehouse that was to have drained him of his memories.

'Then they must have *chosen* the forgetting,' Flugal said.

'We will have the knowing of it when we come to the ice maze at the end of the Coldway,' said Semmel.

Zluty had not really understood until now that the diggers meant to go right to the end of the Coldway, and his spirits fell, for surely it would be quicker and safer to go around the end of the mountains as soon as they could and head West.

He had to get to the Velvet City, for he was sure that was where Bily and the Monster had been taken. Yet for all that, he was curious about what the ice maze could be.

He asked Flugal, when the digger had taken Semmel's place to eat.

'To be mazed is to be confused,' Semmel called from the rim, rather mysteriously.

Flugal took the bowl of porridge he was offered, and began to eat.

Zluty stretched his hands out to the embers of the fire. 'What if the ice maze is what took the diggers memories away.'

'It is not a Makers machine if it is made of ice,' Flugal said.

'Maybe it is *in* the ice,' Zluty replied.

When Flugal returned to the rim, Zluty went to where Semmel was sitting at the side of the vessel, looking forward alertly.

'Did you learn anything more from the memory scents about the beast that took Bily and the Monster?' he asked her.

'Only that it was sent by the Makers,' Semmel said, turning to adjust a bit of the wing.

Her words made Zluty think of his dream.

When the egg voice had spoken in the past, it had given calm instructions or advice or information. In dreams, it always seemed to offer warnings. This time, it had talked of him and Bily saving the world. He almost laughed at the silliness of it, and yet the voice had been so sad.

Zluty went to count the firenuts. They only had six left. Enough to cook three hot meals, if they had enough food.

'How long do you think it will take us to get to the ice maze?' he asked Flugal, who was standing at the front of the vessel, gazing out. 'Another day?'

The he digger flicked his ears. 'There will be no more days until the Longful Night ends.' He turned and ran up the awning frame to shift a bit of wing cloth.

Sighing, Zluty used the coldwhites he had melted and warmed in the ashes to wash the bowls and the porridge pot, thinking that Bily would have made some pancakes as well, getting two meals from one fire.

The thought of his brother brought tears to Zluty's eyes. His greatest fear was that the Listeners would put Bily into their machines and empty his head out, just as the Monks did to the diggers they caught. The possibility that he would find Bily in the Velvet City, only to have his brother look at him blankly, made him feel ill.

He scowled as he dismantled the cooking table and rolled the heavy top bit into its slot, telling himself firmly that the Monster would not let that happen.

He went to join the diggers, who were sitting together on the front of the awning frame, gazing forward. The wind was much stronger now, and they were moving swiftly. He pulled himself up onto the rim beside them and the three of them sat looking out into the darkness as the vessel carried them ever North through the Longful Night.

The perilous journey he made across the ice maze returned often to Bily in dreams.

He would be stepping onto an icy floe, which would tilt as he stepped from it to another slippery floe, and then there would be the sickly rocking as he stood or kneeled or lay on his belly until it steadied under him. He would hear the cold, grinding of ice against ice and the gulping gurgle of the dark water, waiting to swallow him.

Sometimes in the dreams Bily made it safely to the circle of ice peaks that ringed the Hidden Place.

Other times, he would overbalance and fall backwards, landing on the edge of the floe, which would tilt up while he scrabbled desperately for a hold. Then he would slide silently into the freezing black water, and the floes would close over him, trapping him under the ice. He would see Seshla, and sometimes Zluty and the diggers dimly through the ice floe, desperately trying to lift it or gouge through it. And he would hold his breath as he had done in the flooded cellar, until he could hold it no longer and the frigid, black water of the Edgeless Sea filled him.

Or the dream would be of Seshla slipping and dropping the Monster, who would float down until cold black shadows closed over him.

Bily woke from the first of many such dreams, panting with fear, though he knew at once that he had been dreaming, for he was in a bed and wonderfully warm. He had never been so cold in all his life as after that terrifying crossing. He shuddered to remember the last of it.

There had been a stretch of black water between the end of the ice maze and the mist-shrouded Hidden Place, and Seshla had pointed to a little landing that jutted out absurdly.

'There is an opening there. Get onto a small floe and paddle to the landing using your hands. Go as quickly as you can,' she had urged, as she lay the travois and the Monster down on a floe big enough to hold them, and began to paddle. Bily did as she bid him do, his heart hammering with fear.

Oh, the dreadful burning iciness of the water when he put his hands into it! Then his hands went numb and he could not feel them at all. The numbness frightened him and he had to force himself not to stop. By the time he had paddled to the little landing where Seshla waited, his fingers were as white as his fur and he couldn't climb up the ladder onto the landing.

Seshla carried him up, and at the top she put his hands into her hot mouth until the feeling came rushing painfully back.

Only then did Seshla take up the travois, bidding him follow her as she set off through a tunnel in the ice mountain, dragging the Monster behind her. Before following, Bily had turned, his fingers hurting terribly, squinting against the bitter wind, but the land was lost in the blackness of the Longful Night.

Now, Bily sat up in his bed, and tried to remember what had happened after he had stumbled through the tunnel. It had been very long and cold and it had hurt to breathe. He had thought he would never be warm again. Then, when he had come out the other end of it, not only was it dark, but there was a thick wet mist that filled the air, so that he had barely been able to see Seshla, right in front of him. His mind had been in a kind of numb stupor, so that he had been unable to take in what she was saying.

Suddenly the she Monk had lifted her head to give a long piercing call and then they had been surrounded by a jostle of she Monks who gaped in astonished wonder at him, and in even greater wonder at the Monster lying unconscious in the travois.

'Is it the Changebringer?' one of them had asked Seshla.

'Is he dead?' another asked.

'The Changebringer sleeps,' Seshla told them. 'The Great One bit him.'

The other she Monks had nodded sagely and Seshla bid them lift the Monster from the travois and carry him to Ishla. They had obeyed, bearing him along a path that vanished into the mist.

Then Seshla had looked at Bily closely. 'Perhaps it would be best for you to lie down and rest in my hut. It is close by.'

'I want to go with the Monster,' Bily had told her.

Seshla had laid a hand on his shoulder. 'You were very good with the ice maze, Bily. More sure-footed than many of the Monks that attempt it. But you are cold and tired now. You need to rest.'

'I want to make sure the Monster is safe,' Bily had insisted stubbornly. He blushed, but Seshla had merely nodded, and set off.

Bily had stumbled after her along the path and over what he thought had been a little bridge. His legs had felt strange, his hands hurt and his hearing had been muffled by the time they reached a white domed hut and went inside.

The Monster had been lying on a low, soft, circular bed, and gathered around him were many she Monks.

From their sizes, Zluty assumed they were all older than Seshla, though none were as big as the he Monks of Stonehouse, save the silver she Monk who seemed to be in charge.

All of them turned to look curiously at Bily when he entered, but only for a moment. Their attention was on the Monster.

They held devices to his head, and suddenly he awoke with a growling yowl.

Lifting his head, he had bared his fangs and hissed at the she Monks, his tail lashing, but Bily had seen that he was too weak to do them any harm.

Bily rushed forward with the dim idea of protecting the Monster, and then he was close, looking into its narrow golden eyes.

'Oh, Monster, I am so glad you are awake!' he had whispered.

'Bily,' the Monster sighed in his soft velvety voice, seeming all at once to grow calm. Then his eyes closed and his head lolled back.

'What is wrong with him?' Bily had demanded fiercely. His eyes had found Seshla's. 'You told me the Nightbeast would not hurt him! You said he would wake!'

'And so he did and so he will again,' said the silver she Monk in a rough but gentle voice, patting him reassuringly. 'For now he needs to rest, and there is enough of the Nightbeast's venom in him to ensure it. But there is more wrong with this Listener than weariness, I think.' She looked at Seshla. 'I assume it is the Broken Prince foreseen by the wise ones?'

Seshla nodded. 'It is the Changebringer. The

Great One tracked him. But he was ill when we found him. Bily has been tending him. He is a friend to the Changebringer and a healer, too.'

The other she Monks looked at Bily doubtfully, but the big silver Monk said, 'Of course he is. Do not take any notice of this silly gaggle of youngling healers. They cannot imagine a he is a healer because we do not have any among us. What is your name, little healer?'

'I am Bily,' he had told her, mesmerised.

'And I am Ishla, but now I think you must go and rest because I can smell that you are near to sickness with exhaustion.' She turned to Seshla. 'Rider, what do you mean by pushing this little creature so hard?' she thundered.

The other healers shrank back, but Seshla only grinned.

'Keep your fluff on, Oldling,' she answered. 'I offered Bily my own bed, but he insisted on seeing his patient. Now, perhaps he will come with me and lie down.'

'Oldling!' Ishla snapped, but her eyes were full of laughter. Then the she Monk studied Bily rather as the Nightbeast had done, seeming to look beyond his face and into his mind. Her eyes grew serious, but Bily thought they were very kind eyes for all her shouting.

At last, she patted his head again and said, 'Go with that uncouth rider, now, little healer. Sleep. Come see me tomorrow when you are properly awake.'

21

Bily frowned at the little lantern hanging overhead, shedding its soft golden light. It was a round lantern such as the diggers used, and all at once he was certain the diggers that had broken the stone storm machine had come here when they fled North.

He got up. He wanted to go back to the Monster, but he did not know if he could remember the way to the healer's hut. He wondered where Seshla was. He dimly remembered the she Monk ushering him from the healer's hut and along damp and slippery paths through the thick mist, before bidding him crawl through a tunnel into her round, windowless white hut. He remembered falling onto a circular bed, and then nothing but warm, dark oblivion. Until the ice maze dream.

He had the vague memory that Seshla had said she would go and see that the Great One had arrived safely. He had offered to go with her but she insisted he rest because on the morrow he might be summoned by the wise ones and he would need all of his wits about him for that.

Bily thought uneasily of those final words, wondering if there had not been a hint of threat in them. He made up his mind to go outside to see what he could see. He felt very rested, which meant he had slept for a long time, so surely the mist had gone. He was terribly hungry, too, since he had eaten almost nothing since the Nightbeast had taken them, just the ball of dough stuff Seshla had given him.

He crawled out into the open and found it exactly as dark and misty as it had been the night before. But some time must have passed, for he could no longer hear the booming scream of the ice blizzard. He looked up, but could not see the night sky, which meant it was overcast, or maybe the mist had got very thick. Certainly, he felt damp. He could *see* beads of water on the ends of his fur, he realised, because there was a little line of lanterns strung between Seshla's hut and another hut, and then another string that ran to the one beyond. The mist stopped him from seeing further.

'What are you?' asked a voice.

Bily looked down to see a small Monk looking at him curiously. A youngling, though it was almost the same size as he was. To his astonishment, the he Monk had another very tiny Monk sitting on his shoulder.

'I am Bily,' Bily said. 'What is your name?'

'I am Vesh,' the he Monk said. 'This is Zest. He does not talk, but you can hear a little bit of his thinking. Are you the rider of the Broken Prince?'

'I am his friend,' Bily said, knowing he meant the Monster, but puzzled as to what a Prince might be. 'Will you take me to the hut of Ishla, for I need to speak with her?'

Vesh nodded and led him off, saying over his shoulder, 'So you think your friend is really the Changebringer whose coming to the Hidden Place was foretold by the wise ones?'

'I don't know,' Bily said, thinking that Seshla and the Nightbeast had brought the Monster here without asking if it wanted to come, which did not really count as it 'coming to the Hidden Place'.

'Bily,' Seshla said, appearing out of the mist as if his thoughts had conjured her up. 'I was just about to fetch you. Where are these rascals leading you?'

'He *asked* us to bring him to Ishla,' Vesh said virtuously.

'Yes, well, that will have to wait,' the she Monk said. 'One of the wise ones wants to see you, Bily. As I guessed, they are very curious about you and your brother.'

'I want to see the Monster,' Bily said.

'Of course you do, little healer, and so you shall. But he has been taken to the Temple, despite Ishla protesting that he needs more rest.'

Bily wondered what a Temple was. Then he remembered with a chill that the Monster had spoken of a Temple in the Velvet City as being the place where the Makers machines were kept. He had to force himself to mind his manners and thank Vesh for his help. The tiny Monk chittered at him over the youngling's departing shoulder, baring sharp little teeth.

Seshla led Bily along the misty path and over the bridge he thought he remembered from the previous night. But then there was another path and another bridge and more huts, and all of them looked alike, festooned with strings of tiny lanterns.

As they were passing over one bridge, a gust of wind blew and he looked down and saw a little milky-coloured stream running beneath it. Then they came to the edge of a wide pool of water where the mist hung low and very thick. As they came around it, he was astonished to see several Monks sitting up to their necks in the water, some with tiny little Monks like Zest sitting on their shoulders or grooming the fur on their heads.

Bily was so startled that he stopped and stared. 'What are they doing?' he found himself whispering, though he hardly knew why.

'They are wise ones,' Seshla replied, which was not really an answer.

'How can they bear the cold?' Bily asked.

'That water is how we bear the cold here,' Seshla said. 'It is hot, and it streams through the Hidden Place and makes the mist.'

'How do you make the water hot?' Bily asked.

'We do not make it hot, Bily,' Seshla said,

laughing. 'It comes that way from the ground. There are many pools fed by hot streams that rise from deep in the earth. Some are much hotter than this one and some are quite cool. The Great One prefers the Long Pool because it is only warm. That is where she is now, recovering from her icy swim, for even she finds the Edgeless Sea cold. The wise ones like the heat because it eases the aches in their old bones. They spend most of their time in the water during the Winter. On the coldest nights, most of us take to the waters.'

Bily shuddered, then he looked around. 'Where is the Temple?'

Seshla led him further round the pool to where wide pale stone steps ran up into the mist. When he squinted, he could just see that they led to an immense platform where round pillars flanked an open doorway.

Belatedly, he noticed Ishla sitting to one side of the bottom step, eating something. She beckoned them over and bade them sit, patting the step beside her.

'Your friend is being examined by the wise ones,' the big healer told Bily, and offered him some food from a little basket in her lap. There were tiny golden berries piled in a little glistening heap onto small pancakes, and he took one and bit into it. To his surprise, the berries and the pancake were salty, not sweet, but he found them very good once he had got over his surprise.

'Are all the wise ones healers?' Bily asked, taking another of the pancakes when Ishla urged it.

'The wise ones are not healers, though some of them were once. They are not trying to heal the Listener. They are examining his metal. They want to understand how it was broken in the first place so that he was able to leave the Velvet City.'

'I think it got broken *after* the Monster left the Velvet City,' Bily said. 'It . . . he only went off to think about something that troubled him, and then the *arosh* came and drove him East, across the white desert and onto the plain where my brother and I lived. There he was bitten by a blackclaw, and he almost died. I thought he was sick only because of the poison, but the diggers in the camp near the mountains told us the Monster's metal is sickening because of being so far away from the Velvet City, and for so long. We were trying to bring the Monster back when Seshla and the Nightbeast captured us.'

'An interesting story, little healer,' Ishla said, glancing at Seshla. 'But it does not explain why the Listener does not want to return to the Velvet City. This is what interests the wise ones. They want to know how and why his metal broke, so that he can resist its compulsion, even though it hurts him.'

'But he is not the only one to resist it,' Bily said. 'The first diggers resisted their Makers metal when they were upset about the red bird flocks being killed.'

He was not surprised when Ishla nodded. 'We know they broke the Makers machine, not knowing it would also break the binding of their metal to the Makers. But how were they able to break it? That is another thing the wise ones wonder about.'

'There is also the Cloud Monster,' Bily said.

'What is that?' Ishla asked.

So Bily told of the Cloud Monster, and its endless heroic resistance of the Makers pole that had been planted in the high mountains. He got so caught up in his tale that only when he finished did he notice that both Seshla and the healer Monk were staring at him in amazement.

'And you said you were not brave,' Seshla said at last. 'The Great One was right about you.'

Bily wondered what she meant, but the old healer seemed suddenly distracted. She gave him the basket of pancakes and bade him eat the rest. 'That is a very interesting theory of yours about why these creatures have been able to resist the Makers metal in them,' she said thoughtfully.

'Why did the wise ones send the Nightbeast after the Monster?' Bily asked. 'What did they foresee about him?'

'Many of us have dreamed of the Broken Prince who comes North with the means to challenge the Makers and free us from the tyranny of their Plan. We would offer help and advice, if the Change-bringer will act, so that our severed clan might be healed,' said a new voice.

Bily turned to see that several of the Monks in the pool had drawn closer, but it was the nearest that had fastened her gaze on him. She was so old that her fur was white, but her eyes burned darkly.

They want the Makers to stop taking the he Monks, Bily thought. But how was the Monster to help them do that?

He realised with a shock that the old Monk had heard his thought, for her next words were spoken inside his mind. 'If the Broken Prince will submit

to our skills and machines, we will try to change his metal so that it will not bind to the Makers machines when he returns to the Velvet City.'

Bily realised the Monk was offering to ensure the Monster's metal stayed broken. 'If you do that, he need not return!' he cried.

The old Monk shook her head in the bobbing way Seshla had done. 'He must return to the Velvet City for his metal to be restored, but if it can be changed, he will be able to do as he chooses there, and not what the Makers command.'

Bily did not like the thought that the Monster would have to go back to the Velvet City, but at least he could go with them to the Vale of Bell-flowers once his metal had been soothed. Then his excitement dimmed, for clearly the Monks wanted something in return. They wanted the Monster to stop their he Monks from being taken. How could he possibly manage that?

The wise one continued, now speaking aloud. 'What must be done to change the metal of the Broken Prince will be difficult and dangerous for him, and there will be pain. There is danger in it for us, too, for if we are not careful, tampering with his metal will reveal our disobedience to the Makers.'

'But even if you mend his metal so the Makers can't make him do anything, how can the Monster stop them taking your younglings? He is only one Listener, and not even very important.'

'Not important!' cried Ishla. 'The she Listener who gave birth to him is the daughter of the leader of the Velvet City, and he had been chosen to rise higher still – to serve as Prime Listener of the Makers Temple. It is the Prime Listener alone who hears the Makers messages from beyond the sky crack, and who then offers a telling of them to the other Listeners. The Prime is old and the Broken Prince was to replace him.'

Bily was astounded. 'It . . . he said he was not important.'

'Perhaps he *wished* not to be important,' Seshla said gently. 'What I wonder is: Why he did not want to become the Prime, if it would put him so high among his people? Perhaps it is a sign that his metal was beginning to break, even before he left.'

But Bily cried, 'If he was so important, why didn't the Listeners come after him?'

'Maybe they did. But the stone storm would have scoured all traces of his passing. When he did not return, his people probably thought he fell

into a rift and was devoured by *slishi*. Or perhaps they did not follow because they knew his binding to the Makers metal would bring him back,' Seshla said.

'No. Remember that the Listeners do not know that they have metal which is bound to the Makers Machines,' said the wise one. 'They serve the Makers out of love, believing themselves beloved.'

'What will they do to the Monster when he returns?' Bily asked fearfully.

'I imagine his people will rejoice to have him

back,' said the wise one. 'And as long as the Makers do not believe the Broken Prince disobeyed them, but was simply injured, he will be safe from their wrath.'

'Won't his people be angry with the Makers when he tells them about the metal binding?' Bily asked.

'I suspect the Makers binding would ordinarily ensure that he was unable to speak of it,' Ishla said.

Bily looked at the healer, realising what she was saying. 'But if his metal is changed by the wise ones, he could speak of it,' he said. Then another thought occurred to him. 'Only, he could not tell his people the truth then, lest the Makers punish all of them.'

Ishla and the wise one nodded as one.

Bily thought for a bit and then he said, 'If you can make it so the Monster's metal will not bind to the machines in the Velvet City, how is he supposed to oppose the Makers plan if he can't tell his people the truth?'

'He would have great power as Prime Listener,' said the wise one. 'And if his metal is not bound, he can say whatever he likes and claim it as a message from the Makers. He can change the world and no one would doubt him, for the Listeners are highest of all those sent through the sky crack, even if they are not as free as they believe.'

'The Makers will know if the Monster does not tell their words properly,' Bily said. 'And they hate disobedience.'

The wise one nodded. 'That is the difficulty. And yet it must be possible for the Broken Prince to change things, because the dreams say that he brings with him the means for change.'

'It may be that when he is Prime Listener, he will discover how change can be wrought,' Ishla said.

'But before all else, we must change his metal,' said the wise one, sounding suddenly weary. 'If it is possible.'

22

Bily waited on the steps for a long time, waiting to be summoned into the Temple, but finally Ishla suggested he go back to Seshla's hut.

'There is no telling how long it will take the wise ones to complete their examination of the Changebringer,' she said.

The old wise one in the pool, who had seemed to have fallen into a deep sleep, opened her eyes. 'We must speak with the Broken Prince before his examination is complete, and that cannot be done until he wakes,' she said in her cracked voice. 'I will tell the others what I have learned from you.'

Bily realised belatedly that Seshla had brought him here at the request of this wise one, and he was now being dismissed. He hesitated, wanting very badly to see the Monster, but Seshla lay a hand on his shoulder and said that nothing would be done without the Monster's agreement. Even so, it was not until Ishla promised to fetch him the moment the Monster woke, that Bily finally allowed Seshla to usher him away.

She led him in a different direction from the Temple pool, saying they had better go and get some food from the cooking huts.

'I ate all of those pancakes,' Bily protested, but the she Monk said the food was to take back to her hut.

'All meals are prepared and usually eaten communally,' the she Monk explained, pointing to tables with bench seats that were set around the hot pools. They were all empty and mist was swirling around them. Then she pointed to a cluster of three domed huts just beyond the tables. 'Those are the cooking huts. When an ice blizzard is brewing, as now, everyone takes enough food back to their huts to eat over several days.'

'Several days!' Bily murmured, thinking of Zluty and the diggers.

'Do not be afraid,' Seshla said, mistaking his anxiety for fear. 'The Hidden Place is mostly protected from mainland weather by the ice peaks, but it is better to be ready for the worst.'

They waited for the Monks cooking to prepare what the she Monk had requested, and by the time they carried off the baskets of food they had been given, it had grown much colder. Gusts of wind swept along the paths and under the bridges, making the mist churn and roil.

Bily was glad to get inside Seshla's hut, and had just begun to get warm when he heard someone coming along the tunnel entrance. Thinking it might be Ishla or a messenger from the wise ones to tell him that the Monster had awoken, his heart began to hammer with excitement. But moments later, a strange young she Monk crawled into the hut and stood up.

Bily gazed in amazement at her, for she had very long fur on the top of her head, which she had pulled up into a great unruly tree. Some of it was braided, and upon these pieces she had hung a multitude of ornaments. Her pelt had been trimmed to the skin in patterns that coiled around her face and her arms and around eyes that were a deep violet brown that reminded him of the Monster's tail tip and paws touched by firelight. Indeed there were several bits of hair that seemed to have been painted red!

Bily was so busy staring at her that it took him a moment to take in that she was also staring avidly at *him*.

'Ishla asked me to come and tell the mysterious Softling everyone is gossiping about that she has decided to go and sleep in the Temple to watch over the Changebringer. She said to tell you that she has not forgotten her promise,' the she Monk said. 'I do not know what she meant, but perhaps you do.'

Bily was still too dazzled by the she Monk to answer sensibly, because he had never imagined a person might decorate *themselves* as if they were a wall hanging or a clay pot.

'Now look what you have done! You have stolen his voice away,' Seshla scolded the newcomer. The two she Monks glared at one another, then they burst out laughing and hooted and capered uproariously.

'Bily, this is my friend, Finnla,' Seshla said, when

they had calmed down. She clapped the other Monk on her shoulder and grimaced. 'You are covered in snow, you great silly! Look, it is melting on my rug!'

'It is falling outside,' Finnla said absently, gazing raptly at Bily, but she let Seshla take her cloak from her. Bily was enchanted to see the lining was woven in gold and yellow strands that reminded him of Zluty's pelt. Shyly and with a pang of longing for Zluty, Bily stroked its softness while the Monks exclaimed at how rare it was to have a Long Night begin with an ice blizzard, and now here was a second brewing and snow falling on the Hidden Place.

Seshla invited the she Monk to have a bite to eat and Finnla sat down promptly. To Bily's delight, another of the very small Monks – even smaller than Zest – crept out of the bag Finnla had set to one side and crawled into her lap. Seeing his interest, she picked the tiny creature up and held it between them. It looked as her intently as she made a little chittering sound.

'Her name is Wisp,' she told Bily, and bid him hold out his hand.

Bily obeyed and made himself still, while he

offered a crooning greeting with his mind, just as he had once done to the birds or diggers when he had lived in the cottage. The tiny creature tilted its head and then leapt into his hand. Finnla looked astonished, but Bily sat very still, enchanted, as she ran up his arm to his shoulder, then scrambled onto the top of his head to sit between his ears.

Feeling the tufts of fluff on his ears being groomed by tiny claws, Bily laughed softly. The sound made the little Monk freeze. She looked down at him warily as if astounded to find there was a person connected to the ears. He did nothing save croon at her with his mind again, whereupon she scampered down to his lap. Finding his tail curled neatly beside him, she gave a chirp of unmistakable delight and began stroking the long thick fluff wonderingly. Suddenly she burrowed into it and arranged it into a sort of nest, which she curled into before coiling her own tail daintily around her.

Bily looked up to find both she Monks beaming at him.

'My little cousin likes you,' Finnla said. 'You are very fluffy.'

Finnla remained with them for several hours, insisting on braiding a bit of Bily's fur and threading in beads. She had a merry laugh, and despite Bily's worries about the Monster and his fears for Zluty and the diggers, he found himself laughing often, especially at her merciless mimicking of the ponderous wise ones in their endless bath. Seshla roared with laughter when she put on one of Ishla's famous tantrums that she said everyone knew were merely drama without any real anger.

Finnla also asked a great many questions about the cottage on the plain and Bily's life there with Zluty. Seshla wanted to know more about the Northern Forest after he mentioned it, but Finnla was interested in his dye-making experiments and pottery ideas. It was lovely to talk about those things, and he regretted that he did not have the paintbox given to him by the diggers to show her. It was not until she was putting her cloak back on in readiness to leave that she mentioned that she made things.

'Things!' Seshla mocked.

'Hush,' Finnla told her, and invited Bily to visit her hut. Then she left, having scooped up the sleeping Wisp and tucked the little creature inside her cloak.

Seshla and Bily cleared away the eating things and then slept for a time, until Vesh came to wake them, saying the Great One was ready to go seeking Bily's brother and his digger friends and wanted her rider.

'You must hurry, the Great One says, because although the blizzard has ended, she smells that another is brewing, and looks nasty.'

They emerged from the hut and Bily was just

pleading to go and help look for Zluty and the diggers when Ishla arrived.

Seshla shook her head regretfully. 'We must go alone else there will not be room for your brother and the two diggers on the back of the Great One. But also, if another ice blizzard is brewing we will have to move fast. Even so, we may need to take shelter for days on end if it catches us before we can return.'

Bily bit his lip.

'Come now,' Ishla said heartily. 'We two healers have weighty matters to discuss! I would like to know more of your potions and you have not yet seen our water gardens. I think they will be of interest to a healer, for there is a section devoted to healing herbs. Also, some of the wise are eager to discuss with you your theory that strong emotions unsettle Makers metal. And what of the Broken Prince? One of the other healers is watching over him now, but we think it will not be long before he wakes and wishes to speak with you.'

Bily sighed and turned back to Seshla to ask, 'Can I at least come with you to visit the Nightbeast?'

'Of course,' Seshla said. 'But you will need a thick cloak. It is desperately cold at the Long Pool.'

Once Bily was rugged up to her satisfaction, and she had got her own cloak and Riders' bag, Seshla asked the healer if she would like to go with them.

Ishla shook her head, shuddering. 'It is too far and too cold for my old bones. Come to me when you return,' she told Bily, and departed.

'Let's go,' Seshla said. Then she added softly, 'Ishla's bones are only old when she does not want to do something. The rest of the time she is outraged if anyone suggests she is not as fit as when she was a rider.'

'*Ishla* was a rider of the Nightbeast before she was a healer?' Bily asked as they made their winding way through the settlement.

'Not just a rider,' Seshla said. 'She was a First Rider, even as I am. The truth is that she avoids the Great One because it hurts her that they are no longer together. I can imagine how it must feel, not to be able to ride and roam beyond these white walls that are our cage and our protection,' she added a little bleakly.

'The Great One must be very old,' Bily murmured.

Bily and Seshla made their way out of the mist-shrouded Monk settlement along a road that ran North across a coldwhite plain. The mist thinned outside the settlement. Seshla said this was because there were only a few hot pools on the plain. Beyond the plain, Bily could now see the wall of ice peaks and was startled to realise how big the island was. It was also much colder and he was glad Seshla had insisted they wear thick cloaks.

The one he was wearing had been borrowed from Vesh, and Bily had promised the youngling he would return it.

'It doesn't matter,' the he Monk had said, and for the first time the brightness in his face had dimmed. 'When I go to serve the Makers, I will not remember the cloak.'

That was the moment Bily wished the Monster *could* stop the Makers. They had killed Redwing's kind and emptied the minds of countless poor little diggers, and now Vesh and all the other young he Monks were to be turned into the great aggressive Monks that had taken Zluty captive in Stonehouse. The worst of it was that the he Monks would not even have the memories of their youngling days to comfort them as they endured the cold hard life that awaited them. Nor could they refuse to go even if they wanted to, because any rebellion would bring the wrath of the Makers down upon their people.

'How are the young he Monks taken from here to Stonehouse, and how are they made to forget their home and families?' asked Bily.

'There is a machine in the Temple,' Seshla said. 'It tells us which are to be taken. They are always the brightest and cleverest and strongest. Many are those passed over earlier, so that they can stay and sire younglings. When they are chosen, their memories are drained from them by the Makers machine and they are put into metal eggs and taken to the altar on the edge of the mainland. The he Monks and Listeners come after the Long Night to collect them.'

Bily felt sick. 'You would allow that to happen to Vesh?'

'Allow!' Seshla's snaky tail lashed. 'I would fight to keep him and all of those taken, but I can no more do that than Vesh can refuse to go, because the Makers would destroy the Hidden Place if they thought we were not compliant.'

Bily felt ashamed. 'I did not mean to judge.'

The she Monk sighed.

'I judge myself. Yet it may be that Vesh will be

saved, if your Monster agrees to help us.'

'But whatever the Monster will do, that will not save Vesh if his memories are already taken.'

'We secretly keep the memories taken in our vaults. They could be put back into him,' Seshla said quietly, looking at him sideways.

'Scent memories!' Bily said.

The she Monk nodded, looking surprised. 'Did Ishla speak of them to you?'

Bily shook his head. 'The diggers who are descended from those that destroyed the stone storm machine have the scent memories of their ancestors who fled North. They must have learned how to make the scent memories here.'

Seshla shook her head. 'The rebel diggers did come here, but they taught *us* the making of scent memories. It was after we were sent to this Hidden Place by the Makers, and after Stonehouse was built, that the diggers came. In a way, they planted the seeds of rebellion in us. Before that, my people did not question the Makers plans.'

'Why did you take the diggers' memories?' Bily asked.

'We had no choice. They wanted to return to their clans, but they knew if they were captured by he Monks or the Listeners, they would be made to talk about us. We took their memories using the same machine that is used to take the he Monk's memories. But the diggers first showed us how to preserve their memories, and when we released them on the mainland, they carried them in neck pouches. All we did was tell them how to ensure that the scent memories would not wake until they were carried North again.'

Bily wanted to ask what the Monks would do if the Monster refused to go to the Velvet City and become Prime Listener, but he saw a huge pool ahead. Its black water was warm enough to give off a soft mist that hung above the surface of the water, but it was not thick, and through it he could see the island narrowed and stretched out in a long finger that appeared to push through the ice peaks. The path they had been following ran round the edge of the pool and along the finger, vanishing into darkness.

Bily guessed this must be the Long Pool, and the finger of land really did cut through the ice peaks, because that was the way the Nightbeast reached the sea. He wondered where she was. Then she opened her green eyes and he gasped to see she was lying in the water right in front of him, submerged up to her neck. Her strange shifty pelt shone dark as the water.

'Greetings, First Rider, little Softling,' she said very formally to them in her furry voice.

Bily bowed as Seshla did, thinking how he had always imagined the Monster's voice would be brown, if it were a colour. The Nightbeast's voice was darker – a deep purple, almost black.

She stood, and water poured in great noisy cascades from her midnight fur as she stepped onto the bank. Steam rose around her in a cloud, and when she shook her head, scattering droplets, Bily stepped back hastily, unable to repress a shudder at the thought of being so wet, even if the water was warm. When the Nightbeast had shaken herself thoroughly, her fur was nearly dry. He was fascinated to see it was also beginning to lighten because she was standing on cold fluffs.

'I wish I could come with you,' Bily said wistfully.

'Of course you do, little Softling,' the Nightbeast said with a chuckle that tickled his mind. 'But you will be safer here.'

'Wouldn't it be better for you both to wait until this blizzard ends before you go out?' Bily asked.

'It would,' Seshla answered. 'But each blizzard will get worse and we do not want to risk your brother getting West of the mountain range before we find him because the Listeners have planted devices that carry what they see to the Makers.'

'Thank you, Great One, for helping find Zluty and the diggers,' Bily said solemnly.

'I prefer your name for me, Softling,' the Nightbeast said. 'It is lighter than Great One, which is heavy with awe and sits like a stone on my head.'

Seshla made a little mocking bow. 'Henceforth you shall be called Nightbeast. A proclamation will have to be issued about it when we return, for you must not be burdened so cruelly with awe.' Her eyes were laughing and the Nightbeast swatted playfully at her rider with her enormous tail.

Seshla said goodbye to Bily then, and bid him hurry back to the settlement, but he lingered to watch her mount the Nightbeast. They set off at once around the pool and he tried to imagine them coming to the end of the finger of land, where Seshla would dismount and board one of the little floating vessels moored there. She had told him these were used to take the eggs containing the Monk younglings to the place where they would be collected by the Listeners. She would paddle along in the wake of the swimming Nightbeast to the mainland.

Only when they had gone out of sight, did Bily turn to make his way back along the path to the Monk settlement, hidden in the mist at the wide Southern end of the island.

23

Finnla found Bily wandering lost among the huts.

'You should not be outside with a blizzard looming,' she said.

Bily looked up to see that most of the sky was now starless black.

'I have been wandering in circles in the mist, and then I could not find anyone to ask the way to Ishla's hut,' Bily said. 'Will you show me the way?'

'Ishla sent me to find you,' the she Monk said, taking his hand. 'She was summoned to the Temple. The Broken Prince woke and is asking for you.'

As if it felt his shock, the wind gave a long mournful moan and then there was a strange shuddering in the air.

'We should get inside,' Finnla said.

'I must go to the Monster!' Bily cried.

'Very well then, ride and I will run!' Finnla said, and there was a wildness in her smile as she caught him up and swung him onto her back. Bidding him hold tight, she dropped to all fours and began to run, moving at an astonishing speed through the swirling white world between rows of domed huts and over small bridges strung with swinging chains of lanterns.

When they reached the mist-swathed Temple pool, Finnla stopped at the steps and lifted Bily down. He thanked her, noticing to his surprise that the pool was now crowded with Monks of all ages.

'As I told you, when the ice blizzards come, most prefer to take to the hot pools for company as well as warmth,' Finnla said. 'I will bathe myself, now that I have got you here.'

'Aren't you coming in with me?' Bily asked.

'I was not asked and no one enters the Makers Temple who has not been summoned with the knowledge and permission of the wise,' she said.

'Ishla will be waiting inside.'

Bily mounted the long wide steps. He felt suddenly reluctant to go into the Temple, though he could not have said why. Perhaps it was simply that, because of the mist, he could not see the top until he reached it, and then he saw that the four great pillars holding up the roof ran up into further whorls of mist. Peering through the columns, Bily saw an enormous doorway. He looked back down the steps, but could see nothing. It was as if he had entered some strange world lost inside the mist.

Bily gathered his courage and passed between the pillars, but he stopped on the threshold of the doorway. It was bigger than the biggest Monk would need, and he wondered if it was built for Makers. The thought frightened him so much that he had to force himself to go through it. The hall he entered was dark and curved out of sight, but there was light somewhere ahead. He padded along the hall towards it, passing more enormous open doorways leading to darkened rooms either side. It was very quiet and terribly cold and when he looked back, he could no longer see the front door, though he could still hear the muted keening of the wind outside.

'Bily!' Ishla's voice boomed, making his heart jump with fright.

The big she Monk was standing just ahead, holding a lantern. Bily quickened his pace, noticing that the healer was wrapped in a thick cloak. It was no wonder, for it seemed to Bily that it was colder inside the Temple than outside. Approaching her, he saw there was another dark doorway beside her.

'Finnla said the Monster is awake,' Bily said.

'I am sorry,' Ishla replied. 'The Broken Prince did wake, but he fell back to sleep. The wise were able to speak to him, and assure themselves that he truly is the Broken Prince. He asked for you.'

'I got muddled coming back from the Long Pool,' Bily said. 'What did the Monster say about changing its . . . his metal?'

'He said he would allow it, but first he wanted to speak with you. That may be because there is no telling what effect it will have on him.'

'I don't understand,' Bily said. 'You said it would stop him having to obey the Makers commands when he went back to the Velvet City.'

Ishla gave Bily a long look.

'What the wise would attempt is no small thing, little healer. It is dangerous, and they have made sure the Broken Prince knows that.'

'But he won't die?' Bily said.

'Unlikely,' Ishla agreed. 'You see, it is his mind they will be dealing with. That is where the Makers metal is embedded, and a mind can be hurt while the body stays healthy.'

'Hurt,' Bily echoed.

'In order to reach the Makers metal, the Makers machine must be guided on a delicate journey through the brain of the Broken Prince. If they make a mistake, he may forget some things, or everything, for a time or forever, and he might be affected physically, because it is the mind that moves the body. He might be unable to speak, or his sight may be affected, or he might be unable to walk.'

Bily felt sick, but he only asked, 'Can I see the Monster?'

'I will take you to him,' said the healer, gesturing to the darkened doorway. 'Perhaps your presence will rouse him again, or at least let him sleep more serenely.'

'He is sleeping badly?' Bily asked, following the healer through the empty room and into another very large room lit by a number of dim lanterns. This too was empty save for a round mattress upon

which lay the Monster. Ishla went across to him and held the lantern up so that they could peer into his face.

The Monster writhed and growled softly, but did not wake.

'It is dreaming,' Bily said. He, Bily reminded himself, and suddenly he could not see for tears.

'His dreams torment him,' Ishla agreed, when the Monster's paw twitched and twitched again.

'Can I sit with him?' Bily asked.

'Yes, little healer,' said Ishla, laying a big, gentle hand on his shoulder. 'I think it will comfort him to have you close by, for his first waking thought was of you. That interested the wise, for as a rule Listeners care only for their own kind and for the Makers. It seems to us that the love the Prince has for you grew in the broken place. I will return in a while.'

Bily climbed onto the round bed and, when Ishla had gone, he put his arms around the Monster, kissing his head and loving him, because that was all he could do.

Somone tapped Zluty hard on the cheek with a cold finger and he opened his eyes.

It was dark and he was lying flat on his back on the frozen ground. The air was chilly and damp with mist he could not see. There was another hard tap, this time on his forehead, and he winced even as another struck his neck. Belatedly, he realised frozen coldwhites were beginning to fall.

That alarmed him, though he could not quite think why. His head hurt terribly and that made it hard to think. He tried to remember where he was and what had happened, but his last clear memory was of sitting in a coldwhite cave listening to the blizzard roar and keen. But even as this thought came to him, he had a fleeting memory of racing directly towards the mountains, hauling the vessel behind him. Had that happened or was it a dream?

He forced himself to sit, and groaned as a spike of pain shot through his head. His arm hung limp and hurt horribly. He knew at once that he had broken it, but how had it had happened? Had he fallen running and broken his arm?

Getting to his feet, he tried to hold his arm so it would not swing. His head spun and he staggered slightly, dizzy and sick to his stomach. But when he straightened, relief washed over him at the sight of the vessel standing a little distance away. A lantern hung between the tattered remnants of the wing portions, giving out a soft halo of light. There had been another lantern hung on the broken pole sticking out the front, but that had gone.

Zluty limped to the vessel, only to find that it had run up against a great chunk of Makers metal half covered in ice. The collision had stove in the front of the hull and buckled the rim so that it was cracked open. This had sent other cracks spidering around both sides of the vessel and under it. One of the staves had been splintered, too.

Judging from the position he had woken in and the bump at the back of his head, Zluty guessed the vessel had smashed into the Makers device when he was pulling it, wrenching him off his feet. He had fallen hard, breaking his arm and knocking himself unconscious. It seemed impossible that the ice blizzard had turned away at the last minute, and yet it must have done, for he was alive.

He bent to look at the hull more closely, thinking that he could still pull the vessel along carefully if he could get the staves off. Then he realised he could not possibly manage it alone with a broken arm. Bending over had made his head spin and he had to hold onto the vessel to steady himself.

He thought of the diggers then, and a horrible, cold finger of dread ran right down his spine to the tip of his tail. They always rode at the front of the vessel, but there was no sign of them. He went around to open the door and get inside, and the feeling of dread deepened.

They had vanished, just as Bily and the Monster had done. Was it possible the giant beast that had taken Bily and the Monster had returned to take the diggers? But if so, why leave him behind?

He shook his head and the pain made him stagger. He sat down hastily, fearing he would faint, and a fleeting memory came to him of Flugal desperately calling his name. Then there was another awful memory of being trapped in the ground, but that could not be real.

As to the diggers, the most likely thing was that they had awoken and gone looking for the ice chasm the memory scents had shown them. It made perfect sense, and yet he could not believe they would simply leave him lying on the ground. Unless they had not seen him.

He forced himself to his feet and looked out of the vessel to see if he could see the dark bulk of the mountains. He knew they must be close because of the fleeting memory of running towards them, but the mist was so dense and hard coldwhites were falling ever more thickly. He got his staff to steady him, climbed out of the vessel and walked around it in widening circles, trying to find the diggers' tracks before the falling coldwhites covered them.

Then he heard the distant eerie howl that he had come to think of as the hunting call of the ice blizzard. Every instinct screamed at him to leave the vessel and get to the mountains or die. He forced himself to be calm, and went back inside the vessel to push the firemoss into his big forage bag. Carefully, he slung it over his head and positioned it to hang under his injured arm. He pushed the bee urn into it, then lifted his broken arm and rested it atop the urn. Finally, he took up his staff in his good hand and got out of the vessel.

Trying not to panic, he squinted into the windy darkness. He could see nothing. He did the only thing he could do. He set off in the direction the vessel was pointing, pulling his hood about his face to protect it from the falling coldwhites, which were beginning to mingle with sharp ice flowers.

He longed to run every time he heard the muted shriek of the ice blizzard, but he would likely have fainted. He was hungry and cold and his head pounded with pain and fear for the diggers and for Bily and the Monster. But in the end, all of these things, even the grinding pain in his arm that had moved up into his shoulder, were nothing to the torment of growing thirst, for he had forgotten to bring water. After a time, he could think of nothing but getting a drink.

He stopped to scoop up some coldwhites into his mouth and his mind cleared. He realised he ought to have reached the mountains long ago if he had been going in the right direction. Too late, he had a vision of the vessel spinning sideways when it hit the ice chunk.

He stood up, the pieces of ice he had put into his mouth like cold, dry pebbles on his tongue as he turned in a slow circle. A sick dread crept into his heart, for there was no way to know which way to go. Thick white mist swirled on all sides. For all he knew he had been walking in circles from the moment he left the vessel. He ought to have stayed with it. Jammed against the Makers device, it would have offered some protection from the ice blizzard.

He tried to think what to do now, but his head

hurt so much. He heard a strange vibrating sound and a deeper snarling whine. It was louder than before. Closer. He broke into a staggering run, ignoring the pain.

O *Bily*, he thought. *Help me.*

He stumbled over something in the ice, and that was what saved him. He fell hard to his knees, and cried out as the impact jarred his broken arm. For a moment, there was such a blaze of pain the world turned red and fiery, then a strong gust of wind swirled, and the icy coldwhites and the mist parted. He saw by the soft glow of the skystone on his fallen staff that it was sticking out over the edge of a cliff!

Zluty shuffled forward on his knees to the staff, grasped it and stood up. The wind gusted violently, and Zluty saw that he was not on a cliff, but on an icy ledge overlooking a vast white swath of cracked ice floating on a sea of darkness. And he understood. 'I have come to the end of the land,' he whispered, and knew that he was doomed, for the ice blizzard was behind him and there was nowhere to hide.

'Bily!' he whispered as he heard the roar of the ice blizzard and waited to feel its claws.

The mist swirled and parted again and through it he saw shining green eyes coming towards him out of the flying whirl of darkness, from beyond the edge of the world.

Bily was dreaming of someone screaming when Ishla shook him awake, saying Seshla and the Great One had returned.

'Zluty?' Bily had asked, rubbing his eyes.

'They found him, but he is hurt,' Ishla said, glancing at the Monster.

Bily felt as if ice water had been thrown over him. He kissed the sleeping Monster, who had shown no sign of waking, and leapt to his feet. 'Where is he?'

'Finnla said Seshla took him to the healing hut,' Ishla said. 'We ought not to be moving about while the ice blizzard . . .'

'I have to go to him,' Bily said firmly. 'I can find the way.'

'Don't be a fool,' Ishla said gruffly. 'I will go with you, but it will take us time.'

As they made their way through the Temple, the healer explained that they would need to feel their way along ropes that had been strung out along all of the paths, in case anyone needed to move around the settlement. One look at the white maelstrom outside the Temple doors was enough to tell Bily why ropes were needed and why they must wear special thickly padded cloaks to avoid being hurt by the sharp-edged ice flakes.

It seemed to take forever to reach the healing hut, but at last he was inside, and there, exactly where the Monster had lain, was Zluty, looking small and pale. His arm lay at a horrible angle, but other than that Bily could not see any injury.

'It is his head,' Ishla said. 'We think it is cracked. That is very dangerous. We cannot wake him.'

Bily hardly heard her for the roaring in his ears. He went to the side of the mattress and knelt to look into his brother's dear face. Zluty's cheeks were so white that it looked as if there was no blood in him, but when Bily bent to kiss him, Zluty's eyes fluttered and opened.

He blinked and blinked as if he could not focus, and then his eyes fastened on Bily. He frowned. 'Are you a dream?' he asked.

'I'm here,' Bily said in a gasping sob, only realising as he spoke that he had been holding his breath. 'You are safe now.'

He glanced up at Ishla who was beaming and nodded encouragingly.

Bily looked at Zluty. 'I was so afraid for you.'

Zluty made a strangled sound. 'You were . . . were taken by a beast and . . . you were afraid for me?' Then his expression changed and his eyes widened, showing wonder and confusion and fear.

'Bily . . . I came . . . to the edge of the world, and there was a . . . a black sea with ice floating on it, and a huge creature with green eyes came out of it . . . It opened its mouth and I thought it was going to eat me. But . . .'

'It was the Nightbeast,' Bily said. 'It is a she, and she saved you. She was looking for you with her rider, Seshla. It was she who took the Monster. I could not let him be taken so I jumped after him.'

'I was so . . . so frightened when I came back and you were gone,' Zluty said, and now tears ran from his eyes to soak into his fur. 'It was my fault, because I ought to have woken you and told you the diggers had figured out where the Raincage was. They said it was close . . . Oh Bily . . .'

Bily could hardly bear his hopeless jagged weeping. 'Zluty, dear. What is it? What is the matter?'

'The diggers . . .' Zluty managed to say. 'I don't

know what happened to them. I woke up and the vessel was broken and they were gone . . .'

Bily felt a stab of shame that he had not even thought of the diggers.

'We will find them,' he said.

'How?' Zluty asked. 'There is an ice blizzard and there was no shelter. If only I could remember what happened . . .'

Bily stroked his ears and said firmly, 'We found one another, didn't we, and who would have imagined that was possible? All the blizzards and the dark miles and the mountains and the ice maze, yet here we are, together again and safe.'

'Like two hands,' Zluty said, and for the first time, he managed a smile.

Epilogue

Zluty sat on a stone with his cloak wrapped around him, gazing into the dark waters of the Long Pool and thinking that you would never guess it was warm if not for the faint feathers of mist floating over its surface.

He was waiting for the Nightbeast to return. She had gone out again, riderless, to swim. The ice maze had become one vast sheet of ice, now, thick enough to support even her great gliding weight, save for the passage she kept open by swimming it. She had promised Zluty that she and Seshla would go to the mainland to search for the diggers as soon as it was safe. But though there was now a break in the ice blizzards, after they had come thick and fast one after the other for weeks on end, Ishla had explained that during this lull, which the she Monks called the Cold Eye, the sky crack lay directly overhead and the Makers had devices that would let them peer down into the Hidden Place. The Monks had to show themselves to be perfectly obedient to the Makers rules. He and Bily had to wear their cloaks with the hood drawn up at all times outside the huts so the Makers would think they were younglings. Zluty especially must be careful because of the brightness of his yellow fur.

'For all of our sakes, we must not rouse the Makers suspicions,' Ishla had warned.

Zluty had obeyed all of the rules and strictures of the she Monks, not only because there was good reason for them, but, as Bily said, it would have been churlish not to do so when they had rescued him from certain death. Zluty knew that he would have died if the Nightbeast had not spotted him from the water. It shamed him that he had fainted at the sight of it, though Bily insisted loyally that he had been exhausted and injured so it was no wonder.

Zluty could only marvel afresh at Bily's courage, for he had *not* fainted in fear at the sight of the Nightbeast, but had leapt onto the paw of the Monster so that he had been carried away with it into the mountains.

'He is braver than ever I have been,' Zluty murmured. Bily was also far more patient, he thought glumly. He had accepted that they must remain in the Hidden Place for the time being, and had used the time fruitfully to work with Finnla in the water gardens and learn all that Ishla could teach him about herbs and healing. Zluty found it far more difficult to wait, but he had resolved to be patient.

That did not mean to say he liked it. At least he had been able to roam as he liked within the circle of ice peaks, so long as he kept his hood up. And today the Cold Eye would close and the Makers would again be reliant on their machines and their devices to see and hear.

Zluty looked up at the sky. It was dark, of course.

It was impossible to imagine the Makers peering down at him through the sky crack, as they waited for it to be made large enough for them to fit through. How it was being enlarged, Zluty still did not know, nor did the she Monks, save that it had something to do with what the he Monks were doing in the mountains, and something to do with the Listeners in the Velvet City.

Zluty's thoughts turned to the Monster. Zluty had always guessed it had secrets, but he could never have imagined the Monster was so important to its people, nor that it had been fleeing its importance. He was less interested in this, however, than that the duty it had refused was to be Prime Listener of the Velvet City, whose task was to hear the Makers speak.

It did not seem to have occurred to Bily that if the Monks were not successful in changing the Makers metal, the Monster would have to return to the Velvet City where it would again fall under the power of the Makers.

Would the Monks allow it to leave, knowing it was likely to be forced to speak of what really went on in the Hidden Place? Zluty thought it quite likely they *would* let the Monster go, trusting to their foretellings that it would bring change.

Neither they nor Bily seemed to have considered that change did not necessarily mean change for the better. And, of course, Zluty had not uttered that dark thought. Nor an even darker thought that it would be better for all of them if the Monster died or forgot everything when they tried to change its metal, rather than live to betray them if their attempt failed.

Poor Bily spent every moment he could with the Monster, for once it woke and was given to the Makers machines, there was no telling how long it would take to reach its metal and change it, if it could be changed, and then for it to recover afterwards, if it survived.

'*Him,*' Zluty muttered.

Bily insisted they follow the she Monks' customs and refer to one another as male or female, even though Zluty thought it was silly. What difference did it make to them that the Monster was a *he* or the Nightbeast a *she*?

Zluty's gaze was drawn back to the gap in the ice peaks, which led to the black ice-bound sea surrounding them. Bily had explained that the Nightbeast kept a passage to the mainland open through the ice by swimming backwards and forwards along it each day, after which she came to thaw her bones in the Long Pool. That was why he had got in the habit of coming here between blizzards, to wait. It was ridiculous, he knew, yet he could not help hoping every time the Nightbeast went out, that the diggers would come to the edge of the land as he had done, and that she would one day come swimming back with them perched on her head. Or even with news of them – tracks or a distant sighting of them moving across the land.

Wearily, he tried again to remember what had happened before finding himself flat on his back with a broken arm and a cracked head. There was that one memory of running towards the mountains hauling the vessel after him, and a faint memory of Flugal calling out to him for help, followed by the strange feeling of being trapped in the earth. That last one could not be a memory, but Ishla thought it might be a foretelling.

Zluty squinted at the causeway, trying to make himself see through the shadows gathered there, knowing it was pointless. The Nightbeast was always hard to see because of the way her fur shifted colour to match wherever she was standing.

He heard a distant strain of music and sighed.

The Monks were preparing for a festival they called The Waking of The World's Dream, which was to take place once the Cold Eye closed, in the brief lull before the ice blizzards returned for the second half of Winter. Bily had told him the Monks would dance in special finery and there would be music and feasting, but Zluty had not really taken in exactly what was being celebrated. He had asked what the World's Dream was, and had formed the impression it was some sort of display of sky-fire, but surely that could not be right. He ought to have asked more questions, but somehow his curiosity had withered with the loss of the diggers. Indeed, their fate was the only thing he wondered much about.

He longed for the end of the Winter, when he would be able to leave the Hidden Place and go to the mainland to search for Flugal and Semmel, and perhaps to find and repair the vessel.

'Goldsong,' he murmured. That was the name he had thought of calling it, but when he remembered his last sight of the poor broken and bedraggled vessel that had brought them so far, he doubted there would be anything of it left to bear a name.

He sighed again, and this time his breath came out in a little cloud of white. It was getting colder. He heard the crunch of ice and turned to see Bily emerging from the constant mists that flowed out from the settlement.

'I thought I would come ahead,' Bily said, when he reached Zluty's side.

'Ahead?'

Bily smiled at him and pushed back his hood. 'The Cold Eye has closed and the festival is to take place here. The feast is being put into baskets now, and fires will be lit. There will be singing and dancing.' He took Zluty's pipe from his cloak, and handed it shyly to him. 'I thought you might play, too.'

Zluty bit back the impulse to say he could not play music while the diggers were in danger. It was not Bily's fault he had lost them. Zluty blamed himself.

Bily had always been good at hearing things that were not said, and he sat down on the stone and put his arms about Zluty's shoulders, pushing back his hood.

'We will find them,' Bily promised. 'The Monster will wake and we will find the vessel and fix it and go on, and we will find the Vale of Bellflowers and build our new cottage.'

Zluty looked at him. 'You are so sure?'

Bily shook his head, looking up at the sky. 'I am not sure of anything ever, Zluty. But I must hope, for if I do not, then there is only despair.'

Zluty stared at his brother, then he drew a deep breath, and reached out to take the pipe from Bily's hand.

'What song shall I play?' he asked.

But Bily was not listening. He rose, gazing open-mouthed at the sky, a strange greenish-gold light playing over his face. Zluty looked up too, and then he stood, gaping at the immense, shimmering curtains of light hanging right across the sky, undulating as if blown by a wind from the stars.

'Is it the sky crack?' he whispered.

'It is the *World's Dream*,' Bily said, his face shining.

THE KINGDOM
OF THE LOST

The Kingdom of the Lost is a magical series for younger readers from the award-winning author of the Little Fur books.

In *The Red Wind*, a devastating red wind sweeps across the land. Brothers Bily and Zluty are forced to fight for their survival and journey into the perilous unknown to find a new home.

About the Author

Isobelle Carmody began the first of her highly acclaimed Obernewtyn Chronicles while she was still at high school, and worked on the series while completing university. The series, and her many award-winning short stories and books for young people, have established her at the forefront of fantasy writing in Australia and overseas.

Little Fur, Isobelle's first series for younger readers, won the 2006 ABPA Design Awards. *The Red Wind* was awarded the 2011 CBCA Book of the Year Award for Younger Readers.

Isobelle divides her time between her home on the Great Ocean Road in Australia and her travels abroad.

Acknowledgements

I want to thank my lovely editor, Katrina Lehman, for helping me to hone the words that shape this story, and the gentle, talented Marina Messiha, for her tender, creative handling of my pictures. I would also like to say a particular public thank you to my partner, Jan Stolba, for his generous enthusiasm for my artwork, and his endless uncomplaining trips to the photocopier or to buy more nibs, ink and good coffee to fuel me for my night works.